"How are you handling your son's arrival on your doorstep?" Mark asked.

Shannon turned back to him. "Have you looked at me tonight? I'm not handling it that well."

He *had* been looking at her. He could barely take his eyes off her. "I think you're doing all right. It's a lot to digest."

"You act as if it came as a big surprise to me that I had a child." A sad smile spread on her lips. "Believe me, I never forgot it."

"But you never expected him to show up on your doorstep like an overnight delivery, either."

"No. That I didn't expect."

Suddenly Shannon lifted her head and looked right at him. She seemed to be searching for something. Was she trying to decide whether he was just being polite or if he really wanted to know her story?

He was surprised to realize that he did want to know. More than he had any right to.

Books by Dana Corbit

Love Inspired

A Blessed Life
An Honest Life
A New Life
A Family for Christmas
  "Child in a Manger"
On the Doorstep
Christmas in the Air
  "Season of Hope"

A Hickory Ridge Christmas
Little Miss Matchmaker
Homecoming at Hickory Ridge
*An Unexpected Match
*His Christmas Bride
*Wedding Cake Wishes
Safe in His Arms
Finally a Mother

*Wedding Bell Blessings

DANA CORBIT

started telling "people stories" at about the same time she started forming words. So it came as no surprise when the Indiana native chose a career in journalism. As an award-winning newspaper reporter and features editor, she had the opportunity to share wonderful true-life stories with her readers. She left the workforce to be a homemaker, but the stories came home with her as she discovered the joy of writing fiction. A Holt Medallion award winner and Booksellers' Best award finalist, Dana feels blessed to share the stories of her heart with readers.

Dana lives in southeast Michigan, where she balances the make-believe realm of her characters with her equally exciting real-life world as a wife, busy mom to three nearly grown daughters and food supplier to two tubby cats named Leonardo and Annabelle Lee.

Finally a Mother
Dana Corbit

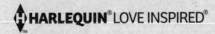
HARLEQUIN® LOVE INSPIRED®

Recycling programs
for this product may
not exist in your area.

 LOVE INSPIRED BOOKS

ISBN-13: 978-0-373-87882-6

FINALLY A MOTHER

www.Harlequin.com

Printed in U.S.A.

Do not judge, and you will not be judged.
Do not condemn, and you will not be condemned.
Forgive, and you will be forgiven.
—*Luke* 6:37

To Ruth Ryan Langan,
you are an example of graciousness and class
in the publishing industry and in real life.
Thank you so much for supporting me, guiding me
and making me believe in myself and in all of those
characters clamoring in my head for their stories
to be told. You are the real deal, my friend.

Chapter One

"Miss Shannon, he just kicked me."

"On my way."

Shannon Lyndon grinned at the sight she must have made, galloping in like the cavalry toward the voice coming from the computer room. The voice of one of *her* girls. The chance that one of them was in any real danger was slim after all. At Hope Haven, a kick didn't necessarily signal an attacker, stomach upset seldom meant the flu and excessive restroom breaks were as ordinary as pop quizzes.

Inside the room, half a dozen teenage girls were crowded around a redhead named Holly. Her chair was pushed back from the computer desk, and hands of varying sizes and skin tones were pressed to her slightly protruding tummy. Most of the girls had rounded abdomens to match hers, and the remaining few would blossom in a matter of weeks.

"He's doing it again." Holly's eyes were as wide as the grin on her freckle-dusted face. She'd already started referring to her child as a "he" although it was too soon for an ultrasound test where she could find out for sure. "Want to feel it, Miss Shannon?"

"Of course I want to."

Well, *want* was a strong word, given that perspiration dotted the back of her neck though late fall already held Southeast Michigan in its frozen fist. And given that no matter how many times she shared moments like this with the teens, she'd never been able to escape her own private longing. But she brushed away the dampness, tucked the lock of hair that had escaped from her braid behind her ear and stepped right inside the circle of teens. One of her girls had invited her into this special moment, and she was determined to be there for every one of them no matter how much it cost her.

It couldn't matter this morning that Holly and the other girls entering their second trimesters weren't the only ones intimately familiar with the butterfly flutter of life inside of them. Shannon's secret was just another square stitched into a faded quilt of memories, and that quilt needed to remain folded away for another day.

She bent over the sixteen-year-old and splayed a hand on her belly. It came as no surprise that she felt no motion beneath her fingertips other than the rise and fall of the girl's breathing. When she shook her head, Holly's smile fell.

"Here, let me try." Kelly, a recent Hope Haven addition with close-trimmed black hair and lovely café au lait skin, squeezed in closer. She held her fingers to the spot Holly indicated for several seconds and then pulled them away. "I don't feel it, either."

Shannon patted Holly's shoulder. "At first you might be the only one who can feel the baby's movements, but before long they'll be strong enough to knock a quarter off your stomach."

"She's right. Believe me." Brooke, in her thirty-third

week, rubbed a spot where a foot or elbow must have been poking her rib cage.

Holly's smile returned as she traced a circular pattern near the hem of her oversize Michigan State sweatshirt. Still a child herself, she clearly was in love with her baby.

Shannon could relate to that. As much to escape from her feelings as to hide them, she turned away from the sweet scene. Only then did she notice the three girls sitting in a row at computer terminals, focused on their online assignments while avoiding the excitement surrounding Holly's pregnancy milestone. It seemed unfair that they couldn't enjoy this celebration of life together since they'd all already chosen life for their babies. But for some of the girls who'd committed to adoption, becoming attached to the fetuses they carried was a luxury they couldn't afford.

Unfortunately, Shannon could relate to that, too.

The girls' varied reactions served as reminders of where they were. No matter how positive she and the other staff tried to make Hope Haven, it was still a Christian home for teen moms. The girls there would make more critical decisions than even the unfortunate choices that led to their pregnancies. Most would make those decisions with no input from their babies' fathers, some without their families' support. Shannon only prayed that the girls would be able to live with their decisions.

"Miss Shannon, have you planned the menus for our Thanksgiving celebration?" Tonya called from one of the PCs across the room.

"We're all set, but the holiday's still six days away, and you have midterms coming up, so don't start thinking about turkey and dressing yet."

Tonya grinned as she tightened the band on her raven ponytail. "Then could you look at this problem for me?"

"Absolutely."

The request for study help came as a relief from the intensity of the moment, that is until she recognized that the honor student was working on derivatives.

"Are you sure you want *my* help? Can it wait until Mrs. Wright comes back to teach on Monday?"

Her ponytail bobbed as she shook her head, her hand resting on the curve of her tummy. "Today you're all we've got."

Tonya probably hadn't intended for her comment to be a monumental statement, but their gazes connected with the truth of her words. While the girls were at Hope Haven, Shannon really was all they had. Well, she and a second social worker, a part-time classroom instructor, a weekends-only cook and a visiting minister, anyway.

Still, her girls were relying on her to help them navigate this terrifying journey into teenage motherhood. They needed her to teach them about proper nutrition and prenatal care, help them keep up with their online high school classes, pray with them, cry with them. And yes, she would even help them with derivatives once she refreshed her memory on how to find those.

"Well, let's give it a shot."

She pulled over a chair and sat next to Tonya, studying the steps the teen had typed below the math problem.

"Wait. You multiplied the coefficient wrong here."

Pushing her red wire glasses up on her nose, Tonya studied the screen and then smiled. "Maybe I should learn to multiply before I take on calculus."

"The simple mistakes are the ones that trip us up."

Shannon pushed back from the desk and stood, grateful that the answer had been easy to locate.

If only the solutions to the challenges facing these teens were as obvious or as simple. Some of the girls and their families would choose to keep the babies, with real or idealized expectations. Several would choose adoption and become the answer to prayer for childless couples. Some would return to their former lives and try to forget this ever happened. But the truth remained that no matter what decisions they made, no matter what justifications they gave for their choices, none of these girls would ever be the same.

Shannon understood that most of all.

The pungent scent of stale ice assailed his senses as Trooper Mark Shoffner passed through the frozen-food section on his way to the Savers' Mart store office. The suspect hadn't picked the most sanitary place in Commerce Township to hit, but he'd been wrong in assuming that the staff would be equally lax on theft recovery.

Inside the office, the juvenile suspect slouched in a chair in a belligerent teen pose: arms and ankles crossed, a Detroit Tigers baseball cap pulled low over his eyes. Mark stopped outside the door, sighing. He'd drawn the short straw again as the new guy at the Brighton Post, having to deal with another James Dean wannabe, especially so early on a school day. If only he hadn't responded to the call from the area dispatcher.

He had to be the biggest misery magnet on the Michigan State Police force. If his cheating ex-wife, who blamed her infidelity on his *marriage* to the force instead of her, wasn't enough, then state cuts requiring the closure of the Iron River Post helped cinch the title for him. With setbacks like these, how was he supposed to build a decorated police career that could prove he wasn't a juvenile delinquent anymore?

Mark referred to his notes from the manager and looked to the boy again. "Blake Wilson?"

"Present."

Blake lifted his hand and let it fall without bothering to look up. He was trying to appear tough, all right. But the coating of filth on his jeans, sneakers and flimsy zipper sweatshirt and the grime melding with the crop of peach fuzz on his chin hinted that the world was beating up on Blake Wilson instead of the other way around.

"Well, good." Mark stepped over the boy's outstretched legs, pulled out a second chair from behind the desk and dropped into it. "I'm Trooper Shoffner of the Michigan State Police. Now, I'll tell you how this is going to go. You're going to sit up in that chair, take off that hat and look me in the eye. Then we're going to have a talk."

"So that's how it's going to go, huh?" The boy continued to stare at a spot on the floor.

"Unless you prefer me to cuff you now and take you on a ride in my patrol car first."

Seconds passed without any movement from the teen, but Mark folded his hands and waited. One of them had to win this power struggle, and it was going to be him. Though they'd only just met, Mark knew the kid well. He'd *been* that kid. But he wasn't that guy anymore, whether others accepted that truth or not, and he needed to stick with the present if he wanted to show the suspect who was in charge.

Finally, Blake straightened and lifted his head, meeting Mark's gaze with intelligent hazel eyes.

"The hat."

Though that gaze flicked to the trooper's hat in unspoken challenge, the boy yanked his cap off by the bill. A mess of greasy dark blond hair fell loose.

"Thank you." Mark left his own cover in place, as state police policy required that troopers wear them whenever responding to a call. "How old are you, Blake?"

"Fourteen."

He bit at skin on the corner of his pinky fingernail and then, switching hands, chewed again. His fingernails were so heavily bitten that it was a wonder he still found anything left to nibble. Just fourteen. Mark jotted the figure in his notebook, guessing that the jaded boy's life experience made him much older than that. "The store manager has reported that you were caught in possession of shoplifted items when you left the store. Can you tell me what happened?"

The boy shrugged. "I was hungry."

The manager materialized in the doorway. "Oh, he was hungry, all right. He walked out of the place like it was a food bank or something."

"Food bank?"

In answer to Mark's question, the man indicated items arranged on a table lining the office's back wall. Something heavy settled in Mark's throat. No cold medicine that could be cooked up into more powerful drugs. Not even a six-pack of beer or a pack of cigarettes. The suspect was accused of swiping a half gallon of milk, a box of corn flakes and a carton of cherry toaster pastries. A teenager's breakfast of champions. Arresting a hungry kid was the last thing he wanted to do, particularly so close to the annual gorgefest that was Thanksgiving, but unpleasant tasks sometimes were part of the job.

He turned to the store manager. "Thank you for your

help. I will be taking Mr. Wilson back to the post for further questioning. I will be in touch."

The trip would also include a breakfast stop at a fast-food restaurant, but Mark didn't mention that to the manager, who would be complaining about special treatment. He'd questioned many things about his new faith that had helped him to turn his life around and then failed to keep his wife from leaving him, but the lesson he'd learned about feeding the hungry still seemed like a good idea.

Soon the suspect was Mirandized, cuffed and seated in the back of the patrol car, and they were headed west on the Interstate toward the post. Well, fidgeting in the backseat, anyway. How Blake had managed to do that with his hands cuffed, Mark wasn't sure, but the boy's wiggling had already caused the blanket that Mark had tucked around his shoulders to fall behind him. The only thing that stayed in place was the hat that Mark had returned to him.

"You're just going to make the cuffs rub your wrists raw," he pointed out.

"So?"

But the squirming stopped for about a minute, and then it resumed as if the boy couldn't control it. Instead of mentioning it again, Mark took the Milford Road exit and headed south toward a shopping plaza with several fast-food restaurants nearby.

"We'll call your parents once we reach the Brighton Post, but I'm hungry, so I'm going to stop for some breakfast." He glanced at the boy in his rearview mirror. "I can pick something up for you if you like."

Unmasked longing flitted through Blake's eyes as he took in the brightly colored fast-food restaurant signs, but he blinked it away as he met Mark's gaze in the glass.

"Can't we just go to my house first? I mean…it's right by here."

Mark wasn't sure which surprised him more, that a hungry teen was turning down food or that the boy was begging to see his parents sooner than he would have been forced to once they reached the post. Since he'd suspected that Blake might be a runaway, he was curious to see just how close they lived.

"Why would you want to go there now?"

"My parents will go ballistic when they hear about me getting into trouble anyway, so we might as well get it over with."

The Lie-o-meter should have exploded on that one because Mark wasn't buying it. The kid had probably figured out that the store was unlikely to press charges. Or maybe he had a juvenile record a mile long and wanted to delay Mark's chance to get back to his computer. Mark's lips lifted at the thought. Blake had missed the laptop mounted on the patrol car's dashboard if he believed a side trip could slow access to that information.

"Good to get it over with." His gaze flicked to the mirror. "Sure you don't want to eat something before—"

Blake shook his head, interrupting him. That settled it. Something was making the boy desperate to get home. Something more powerful than hunger intense enough to drive him to steal. And Mark had to know what it was.

"Okay, what's your address?"

He popped open the laptop and typed the address Blake gave him into the GPS. The short trip led to a rural area near the line that separated Oakland and

Livingston counties. Turning off on a county road, he made a second left onto a lane with only a few houses spaced along it. He pulled onto the narrow drive of an expansive two-story brick house, remarkable in no way beyond its size. The place had seen better days. Its outbuildings were faded. Its gutters hung loose. Its long, blacktop drive begged for recoating. The owner had obviously tried to warm up the place with a fall display of hay bales and yellow chrysanthemums next to the porch, but the effort only reminded Mark of a tiny color portrait on a bare wall.

"Is this it?" At least it was a house. Many of the suspects he'd met lived with less. Far less.

"Guess so."

From the way Blake was looking at the place, Mark could only guess that he hadn't been there in a while. Maybe his premise about the boy being a runaway was right. No need to mention it now, though. He would have answers to at least some of his questions soon.

"Sure your parents will be home?"

"Hope so."

Mark climbed out of the car, put his cover on his head and crossed to the rear door on the passenger side. After Mark had helped him out of the car, Blake looked over his shoulder, indicating his cuffed hands.

"Sorry," he said with a shake of his head.

Frowning, the boy allowed the trooper to lead him up the walk. They climbed the crumbling steps onto the porch, and Mark rang the bell. Female voices filtered through the wood before a young girl pulled open the door. A very pregnant Hispanic teen.

She stared at them with wide eyes. "May I help you?"

"Who is it?" Another teenager pressed in next to her, this one a Caucasian blonde, clearly pregnant, as well.

She shifted her feet, and her gaze slid right to left in that uncomfortable reaction that even innocent citizens sometimes have to an officer in uniform.

"Is it for Miss Shannon?" A third teen, this one African-American with what appeared to be the beginning of a baby bump, pulled the door wider so she could fit into the space.

Finally, the door came fully open, and enough girls to field a soccer team looked out at them, some with open curiosity, others with caution. Most were clearly pregnant.

What had he just walked into? Mark scanned the front of the house, trying to locate a sign, but he didn't see one. He'd had no idea that homes for unwed mothers still existed. Didn't pregnant girls usually walk the same high school halls with other students these days? It was obvious, though, that Blake had played a joke on him by leading him to one of these places out of the past. The kid might think this was funny now, but he wouldn't be laughing when they returned to the station and he booked him.

But when Mark turned to him, Blake wasn't paying any attention to him. He was staring straight ahead, his posture rigid, his chest pushed forward. Mark followed the boy's gaze to the petite brunette who had appeared in front of the girls. And Mark couldn't have looked away if the woman had demanded it with a handgun.

She had this fair porcelain skin, these huge hazel eyes, delicate features and amazing full lips, which combined to give her a fragile, china-doll quality that was just unfair to a guy trying to keep his thoughts on the job. Dressed in jeans and a Henley shirt and with her hair tied back in a braid, she could have been mistaken for one of the girls, but the creases at the corners of her eyes and her attempt to corral the teens behind her signaled that she was in charge.

For several heartbeats, she stared back at him, a deer caught in his headlights, and then, as her cheeks turned a pretty pink, she shifted her gaze to Blake.

Mark cleared his throat. If he couldn't avoid noticing a female while on the job, at least he'd chosen the only adult in the room. She didn't appear to be pregnant like the girls either, he noted, feeling strangely relieved. What was that about?

"May we help you, Officer? Has something happened?" She glanced from Mark to Blake, her gaze narrowing.

He frowned, expecting *idiot* to be stamped on his forehead. Who could blame a woman in a house full of pregnant girls for being cautious when facing a police officer and a teenage boy in handcuffs?

"Everything's all right, ma'am. My name is Trooper Mark Shoffner." He paused, clearing his throat again. "We apologize for the disturbance. There was a mistake about the address."

"Oh... Okay. You must be new. This home is a center for teen mothers. It's called Hope Haven. I'm Shannon Lyndon, the housemother and one of the social workers."

At least she hadn't asked more about why he'd brought a dirty, handcuffed teen to her front porch because he wasn't sure how to answer that. She wasn't looking at him, anyway. She was studying Blake as if he was a science specimen. Finally, she shook her head. Her cheeks flushed again. Mark hadn't noticed earlier, but her hazel eyes struck him now as familiar. Had he met her before? That was unlikely since he'd only transferred to Brighton a month earlier, but he couldn't shake the sense that he knew her.

"Well, thank you and sorry, again, for the disturbance." He backed away from the door, pulling Blake along with him, but the boy dragged his feet.

"Wait." Blake's voice was tight.

Mark stopped. "What's going on? I don't know what you're trying to pull here, but I'm not impressed."

He wasn't happy with himself either, for letting his curiosity get the best of him and for agreeing to come here in the first place.

"I can explain."

"Well, you'd better start. Now. Did you think it would be funny to bring us here? Because this obviously isn't your house."

The boy didn't crack a smile, didn't even look his way. Instead, he trapped the housemother in a straight, accusing stare.

"No, I don't live here." He paused a few heartbeats before adding, "But she *is* my mother."

Chapter Two

Voices all around Shannon erupted in varying tones and speeds, but the words themselves were muffled and faraway. She couldn't think. She couldn't move. She couldn't breathe. *Mother.* The word she'd waited fifteen years to hear spoken in reference to her, the word she carried in her heart, so soft in its potential, its reality full of jagged edges.

But the venom she hadn't expected. Now she didn't know why she hadn't prepared herself for that. She didn't question for a second that this was her baby. Her big boy now. He was standing right there in front of her, dirty, sure, but tall and handsome. She couldn't get enough of seeing him. Eyes so like her mother's… and her own. A face that looked like, well, his father.

Taking in all of him, she couldn't help but notice that his arms were cuffed behind him or that he appeared to be in the custody of a uniformed police officer. One with the heavily lashed black-brown eyes and the short brown hair that showed off the kind of face that could have been—no, should have been—sculpted in marble. Shannon blinked, catching herself staring again. She'd had no business gawking at the handsome officer even before she'd recognized Blake. Now it was unforgivable. What kind of woman allowed a man to distract her at a time like this? Well, someone who'd allowed a guy to sidetrack her in the past from what really mattered. But not this time. She didn't care about the trooper's broad shoulders and strong-looking arms and chest dressed up that navy blue uniform with its silver tie and badge.

She pushed those unacceptable thoughts away and zeroed in on Blake. Why he'd chosen to come here today, how he'd gotten into trouble, even the officer who'd brought him here—none of that could matter. Nothing except that he was here now.

"Blake?" It was the first time she'd ever spoken his name aloud, and she could only manage a squeak. She cleared her throat. "It is *Blake,* right?"

He didn't respond as he stood, shifting his feet, but he didn't look away, either. It was something. She braced herself and accepted the accusation and conviction in his gaze the best she could. He deserved that much, and if he gave her the chance, she would make him understand.

"She had a baby?" someone said in a low voice. "A baby as old as *him?*"

"And he got arrested? That means…"

Whispered questions that escalated to frantic chatter invaded her senses, making her vaguely aware that they weren't alone, but she couldn't bring herself to look away from her son. *Her son.* Just the thought of it made her long to reach out to touch him. When she could no longer resist, she took a tentative step toward him, her hands lifting from her sides.

"Do…not…touch…me."

His words were a wall of glass, keeping her from the only thing she'd ever wanted, the chasm between them suddenly huge and growing. She'd never expected to feel anguish again like the day the nurse had carried her blanketed baby from the birthing room and from her life, but here it was again, bitter and deep. If she could move at all, she would have collapsed into a heap of loss.

"Why don't we take this conversation inside?"

She blinked at the sound of the officer's voice, and her gaze flicked to him. Accusation filled his eyes. His expression was as hard as Blake's was. What right did this stranger have to judge her when he didn't know all the facts of the situation? He didn't even know that the choice hadn't really been hers. But then Shannon shivered as she became aware of the frigid air pouring in through the gaping front door. And that Blake's sweatshirt was so thin.

"Oh. What was I thinking? Sorry."

Backing away from the door, she bumped into Holly right behind her. She whirled to face the shock on so many of the girls' faces. How betrayed they had to feel over learning about her secret this way. They would never understand that it was her shame and not a fear of trusting them with her story that had kept her from sharing it.

"Miss Shannon?"

So many questions were folded into Holly's two words, and Shannon promised herself she would answer every one of them, but she owed her son an explanation first.

"Girls, could you just give me—"

"We're going to need to speak privately with Mrs. Lyndon," the trooper said, interrupting her.

"Miss," she corrected.

His gaze flicked to the bare finger on her left hand.

"Sorry. Miss." Guiding Blake inside, he closed the door behind him. "Ladies, could you give us a few minutes?"

The teens paused, reluctant to leave her alone with the two males.

Chelsea, who had celebrated her fifteenth birthday at Hope Haven just last week, touched her arm. "You going to be okay?"

Shannon nodded, though she was as unsure as the girls appeared to be. "I'll be fine. Just work on your lessons in the computer room. I'll be in as soon as we're finished."

She didn't bother telling them that everything would go back to normal when she returned, if she could call these lives they'd lived on a tangent at Hope Haven "normal." For Shannon and for the girls she worked with every day, nothing would be the same.

Once the door to the computer room closed, she braced herself and faced the officer, the boy and the past that haunted her memories.

Trooper Shoffner guided Blake a few steps forward so that he was standing in front of her.

"I take it you and Mr. Wilson know each other?"

Shannon looked longingly at the boy who'd stared her down earlier but now refused to look her in the eye. "Well, not exactly, but—"

"You called him by name."

"As I started to say, he is, he is…my son." She was simply putting the truth into words as Blake had done, so she hated that her voice broke under the weight of it. She tried again. "I gave up a baby boy for adoption almost fifteen years ago. I met the adoptive parents once. They told me if the baby was a boy, they would name him Blake." She lifted a hand to indicate the teen. "That's him."

"You're certain of this?"

"Look at him. Don't *you* see the resemblance?"

The officer didn't look at either of them as he withdrew a notebook and pen from his pocket, but Blake sneaked a glance at her from beneath his shaggy hair.

"Obviously, maternity will have to be confirmed." He tapped his pen on the paper. "But since you appear to have an interest in this boy, you should be aware that he was arrested this morning. You might be interested in knowing what type of items he was accused of shoplifting."

"Um, okay." Since Blake had turned to his side now, she couldn't help staring at his cuffed hands.

"Food." Trooper Shoffner spat the word as if it had soured in his mouth. "He was hungry."

The officer's censure stung, but not as much as the reality that the precious boy next to her had ever known hunger. How could that have happened? "Oh. You poor thing."

"He also appears to be a runaway."

The trooper's stony expression told her he wasn't kidding. If his first comment had been a stab, he'd twisted the knife with this one.

"Blake?"

His only answer was a shrug. She needed him to look at her, to tell her this was all a mistake, but he kept staring at the ground.

Catching herself this time as her hands lifted to touch him again, she stuffed them into her pockets. "What happened? Did you have an argument with your…parents?" She hated that the word caught in her throat. They were his parents after all. Under the law, she was his birth mother. Nothing more.

"If you give him something to eat, he might be able to answer your questions," Mark said.

"You mean you didn't feed him? You knew he was starving, and you couldn't stop before coming here?"

He met her incredulous look with a steady one. "I started to, but he insisted on coming here first."

Her righteous indignation fizzled. The blame was back on her, right where it belonged.

"Right. Well, take those cuffs off him and bring him in the kitchen."

"I don't think—"

"He can't eat without his hands." She didn't care if she'd just given an order to a police officer, who was clearly more accustomed to giving them than receiving them. For whatever reason, her child was hungry. She might never have been able to do anything for him before, but she could feed him now and help free his hands so he could eat.

The trooper studied Blake for a few seconds and then withdrew a key from his pocket, stepped behind the boy and opened the handcuffs. Blake rubbed his wrists and spread his fingers to stretch them before jamming them in his sweatshirt pockets.

As Shannon led them down the hallway to the kitchen, questions ticked in her mind at the same pace as her tennis shoes on the worn wood floor. Why had Blake run away? How had he known her identity or how to locate her? Had his adoptive parents refused to let him search for her?

In the kitchen, she opened the huge, industrial refrigerator and stepped inside the chilly room to scan the contents. She grabbed a carton of eggs, a green pepper and a tomato and closed the door.

"Hope eggs are okay."

Blake cleared his throat. "Anything's fine. Except tomatoes."

"You'd probably eat even those this morning," Trooper Shoffner said with a chuckle.

"Probably."

But Shannon wasn't laughing, as irrational fear tightened her throat. She was about to make a first meal for her son, ever, and she knew nothing about him. What did he like to eat? Did he prefer video games or TV? Did he have food allergies? Worse than that, she didn't know what type of life he'd led until now or what unfortunate events had landed him on her doorstep.

But she would find out. She would ask her questions and answer his. She would listen, no matter how painful his stories, no matter how much he blamed her. This was what she'd wanted: to be reunited with Blake and to have a chance to explain the past. Although this wasn't the warm and tender reunion she'd imagined and prayed for, this was their story, and they would find a way to work through it. Her son had come looking for her. He was close enough to touch, if he would ever allow it. Having him with her was the most important thing. The only thing.

"Slow down or your breakfast is going to come back up," Mark warned as Blake shoveled food into his mouth with barely a breath between bites.

He'd been right. The boy would have eaten even the dreaded tomatoes, and might have licked the plate afterward, if Shannon Lyndon had set those in front of him at the long table in the house's cafeteria area. Although the boy didn't appear to be malnourished overall, something told him that this wasn't the first time Blake had ever been hungry. The same protective impulse he'd felt when he'd realized the boy was accused of stealing food rose in him again, but Mark tamped it down a second time. Becoming involved in this mess of a situation was the last thing he should do, even if he felt terrible for the boy who was the true victim in it.

Shannon sat across from them, staring in amazement at the boy as he wolfed down his food. She shouldn't have been shocked. She'd known all along he was out there somewhere. Or at least some kid who was about Blake's age. Mark shifted in his seat as the scent of Miss Lyndon's perfume—something light and floral and too feminine for its own good—mingled with scents of Blake's breakfast. Clearly, he was picking up on the wrong details in this case if he was mentally cataloging that one.

"You're left-handed," Shannon said to the boy.

Blake's fork stilled. "So?"

"My dad's a lefty."

"Oh."

As Blake scraped his plate, he met the woman's gaze with those green-brown eyes. Instantly, Mark knew why he'd found Shannon's eyes so familiar. They had to be related.

"Hey, any chance I could get some more?"

Setting his coffee aside, Mark patted Blake's shoulder. "Give the food a few minutes to settle. If you're still hungry after we talk, I'm sure, uh…Miss Lyndon would be happy to give you seconds."

He wrapped his hands around his mug again, frustrated that he hadn't been sure what to call her. He wouldn't refer to this woman as Blake's birth mother without proof, even if he suspected it was true. If she'd chosen to give up her parental rights, she had no claim to Blake, anyway.

"Sure. Whatever you want." Shannon smiled across the table at the boy.

"Now, Blake, let's start with you." Mark picked up his notebook and pen. "I need your parents' names and numbers so I can let them know where you are."

Blake dropped his fork on his plate and pushed back from the table, crossing his arms. "Which ones? Birth parents? Adoptive parents? Foster parents?"

"Foster parents?" Shannon asked.

"And of the foster parents, which of those do you mean?" Blake continued as if she hadn't spoken. "There've been a bunch. Some decent. Some not so much."

Shannon drew her brows together, gripping the edge of the table so tightly that half-moons of white appeared beneath her nail beds. "Wait. How can that be?"

Blake looked up from his plate, trapping her in his gaze. "The state has this thing about parents who neglect their kids. Funny, they think that kids should have a few things. Food. Clothes. A place to sleep."

Shannon shook her head. "No. The couple I met was so desperate to adopt a baby. They both had steady jobs. They could provide anything a child would need or want."

"If not for the drugs."

The anguished sound escaping from Shannon's lips made something tighten inside Mark's gut. He could understand some of the shots Blake had taken with his comments. The boy definitely deserved more compassion than the adults in this twisted situation did. But as this shot made a direct hit, the color slid from Shannon's face like a snow cone once the flavoring was gone.

"You were temporarily removed from your adoptive parents' home because of drug addiction?" Mark couldn't help but watch Shannon as he asked it.

Blake made a flippant gesture with his hands. "The first few times. The state took away their parental rights when I was seven."

"That can't be. It can't be," Shannon said miserably, tears draining from the corners of her red-rimmed eyes. "I was supposed to be doing the right thing. That's what they told me. The best thing."

"You couldn't have known," Mark heard himself saying despite his intention not to weigh in.

Always uncomfortable with crying women, he scanned the room for tissues and crossed to a table near the door separating the dining area from the kitchen to grab some paper toweling instead. She nodded her thanks and dabbed her eyes, her lashes spiky and wet.

He would have reminded her that adoption was often the best choice for pregnant teens, something she had to know from working at Hope Haven, but she wouldn't hear him now. *This* adoption hadn't been the best thing for *this* child. For Blake. He reminded himself who was central to this situation. He couldn't lose focus of that fact no matter how much the tears tracing down her cheeks threatened to soften him with their salt.

"Okay, I need names, an address and a contact number for your current foster parents. We'll contact them and the Department of Human Services when we get back to the post." He wrote down the information the boy provided. "You came all the way from Rochester Hills? That's about seventy miles from here. Did you walk all that way?"

"Hitched some of it."

From the look of him, Blake had crawled the rest. But no matter how he'd gotten there, the boy had come a long way for answers from the woman he believed to be his birth mother, and he would get them if Mark had anything to say about it.

"Miss Lyndon, you said you gave up a child for adoption born when and where?"

"Nearly fifteen years ago. On March 7. In Shelby Township."

He turned back to Blake. "And your birthday is?"

"March 7."

He wrote a check next to the date in his notes. "And you were how old when you gave birth?"

"Fifteen." She sniffed and wiped her cheeks with the towel. "I was sent away to stay with my grandma until he was born."

"And the adoption was conducted through…?"

"A local attorney." She coughed into her hand. "I wasn't exactly given a choice."

Doubt flashing through Blake's gaze, he looked away. The boy was gripping his anger like a precious possession, and he wouldn't give it up easily.

Mark tapped his pen on the pad. "The infant's father?"

"MIA. From the beginning."

Shannon Lyndon's story was a cliché. As common as teen pregnancy. So the sudden rise of his anger at this unidentified deadbeat dad shocked him. He cleared his throat. "Now we have the basics, but, Blake, we need to know how you knew to come here. Adoption records are supposed to be sealed. How did you find out the identity of your…of Miss Lyndon?"

Shannon leaned forward, resting her arms on the table, curious, as well.

Blake pulled something out of the pocket of his filthy jeans and tossed it on the table. The crumpled piece of paper might have once been blue floral stationary, but now it bore only a faint blue hue.

"What is that?" Mark asked.

The boy didn't answer, and Shannon only stared at the piece of paper as if she already knew what it was. Mark reached for it and unfolded it. His throat tightened as he read the smeared words written in a loopy script: "To my dearest baby boy..."

He skimmed the private message, its words those of a brokenhearted girl. At the bottom of the page, Shannon's name and what must have been her parents' Walled Lake address stared back at him, a confirmation in faded blue. He folded the note again and placed it on the table in front of him. Shannon and Blake only stared at each other, her pleading expression unable to breach the wall of the boy's unbending one.

"They were supposed to give you that letter when you were old enough to understand," she said in a small voice.

Her hands reached toward Blake, but then they froze, and she lowered them to the table, gripping them together.

"You trusted people who couldn't even remember to feed a kid to keep a letter like that in a safe place?"

A strangled sound escaped Shannon's throat. "I didn't know."

"Well, you should have."

Shannon must have heard as much as she could bear because she buried her face in her hands. Her shoulders heaved with the force of her sobs. Each shake echoed inside Mark's chest, and he couldn't make it stop. If that didn't shame him enough, his hands itched to reach over and pat her arm. Where was his professional distance when he needed it? Hadn't he already learned the hard way not to be a patsy for duplicitous women?

He pointedly turned his attention away from her and back to Blake. "How did you know to find Miss Lyndon here? The address on the letter says Walled Lake."

"They allow the internet in foster homes, you know. Sometimes they even have wireless."

"Right." Mark chose not to address the wise-guy comment. This time.

When Blake leaned forward and reached for the letter, Mark closed his hand over it. "Sorry. I'm going to need to make a copy of that. I'll give it back later. I promise."

"Whatever."

He shrugged as if he didn't care one way or another, but Mark wasn't buying it. That letter had traveled with the kid through several foster homes for at least seven years. It was probably his most precious possession.

Mark turned back to Shannon, who was wiping ineffectively at her eyes.

"Miss Lyndon, do you have someone you can call in to stay with the young ladies? I need you to come to the post with us to sort out this matter."

"The other social worker, Katie, should be here soon."

"Then until she arrives you might want to speak with your residents." He gestured toward the kitchen door. "They'll probably have a few questions."

"Oh. Right." Bracing her hands on the edge of the table, she pushed back and stood. She started for the door, and then, as if remembering, turned back to them. "Did you still want something more to eat?"

Blake shook his head. "No, I'm full."

Mark doubted that, but after the conversation they'd

just had, he couldn't blame even a hungry kid for losing his appetite. He'd certainly lost his.

"I'll be right back, then," Shannon said.

She paused in front of the door and then straightened her shoulders and pulled it open. Outside, a group of disobedient girls stood like a jury waiting for the foreman to announce a guilty verdict. Shannon froze, her hands stiff at her sides. Clearly, the girls had heard at least part of the conversation because they wore a collective look of shell-shocked fury.

Again, that temptation to protect the woman rose, intense and unwelcome, and it was all Mark could do to stay seated instead of stepping between her and her accusers. It wouldn't have helped for him to tell them that they didn't have as much of a right to their anger as Blake did, anyway. They felt betrayed. It didn't matter that Shannon had been under no obligation to share the truth of her own pregnancy and adoption with a group of teenagers she counseled.

This was a muddy mess, with more than enough smears of anger and blame to cover them all in muck. But in the chaos, one thing had become disconcertingly clear to him: Shannon Lyndon was standing all alone as she faced the mistakes of her past.

Chapter Three

"There's good news and bad news."

Shannon startled at the sound of Trooper Shoffner's voice. She turned as he strode back into the interview room of the Brighton Post and took a seat at a long table against the wall. She had to be jumpy over the officer catching her staring at Blake again because it couldn't be that the man himself unnerved her. It wasn't her fault she couldn't stop looking at her son, even if Blake had no problem ignoring her. Sometimes she could almost feel the boy's gaze on her, but when she would look over, Blake would be fidgeting or biting his nails.

"So what did you find out?" She craned her neck to look through the doorway to the open area of the squad room. The caseworker from the Department of Human Services was still at one of the desks, talking on her cell phone.

"Which first, good or bad?"

"I vote for good," Shannon said, though the question hadn't been for her.

Maybe some good news was just what Blake needed to help him forget about his anger for a while. She hated that he hadn't spoken to her during the car ride, but she refused to give up hope of establishing a relationship with her son. They were together, and she could ride for a long time on the adrenaline of that answered prayer.

"Blake? What do you think?" Mark pressed again.

Whatever Mark had planned to say had him grinning at Blake, but when the boy didn't look up, he turned that smile Shannon's way. Her breath caught. Though she'd noticed the trooper's straight white teeth when he'd spoken earlier, she couldn't imagine now how she'd missed those dimples. And for that matter, how had she failed to notice those intense, dark eyes that seemed to see straight through a person? Even women like her, who'd sworn off men, and those with as much on their minds as she had today couldn't avoid noticing such appealing scenery.

"The bad."

It was Blake's voice that startled her this time. Instantly, she was ashamed. After waiting so long to be reunited with her child, what kind of mother was she to allow her attention to be drawn away from him, even for a second? With her son blaming her for his life after the adoption and with her girls feeling betrayed that she'd kept her secret, she had no time for other distractions. Particularly a man.

"Why the bad first?" Mark wanted to know.

But Shannon suspected she knew why, and that only made the braid of ache inside of her stomach twist tighter. Someone who'd experienced as much bad news as Blake had couldn't trust anything masquerading as good news.

Mark closed his notebook. "Okay, the bad news. Your foster parents reported you as a runaway, which adds to a pretty impressive juvenile record. And because you did run, they have refused to let you return there. You'll be a bad example for their other foster children."

"No big loss."

"No big loss?" Mark repeated his words.

Blake lifted a bony shoulder but didn't look up from his hands. "Is that it?"

Shannon exchanged a quizzical look with Mark but managed to hold back her own questions. Why didn't Blake see the rejection of his current foster parents as a loss? Had they abused him? Assumptions crowded her thoughts, each one more horrific than the last. Then the realization struck her that whether or not that couple had hurt him, others probably had. Worse than that, she was responsible for placing him in the care of his first abusers.

"Miss Lafferty's out there right now, working with the private agency responsible for your initial foster placement. They're looking for another one," Mark continued.

I'm right here, Shannon wanted to shout. It was difficult to think of another placement for her son besides with her, but her social-work training told her it wasn't so simple. She hadn't proved yet that she was Blake's birth mother, let alone that she could properly care for him.

"Have fun with that." Blake's chuckle held no humor.

Now Shannon couldn't stop herself. "What do you mean, 'Have fun?'"

"I'm what they call a 'placement challenge.'"

"Why?" She tried to ignore that he'd spoken to Mark instead of her.

"ADHD." This time Blake stared directly at her as he spat the acronym for Attention Deficit Hyperactivity Disorder. He seemed to have forgotten that he hadn't sent a single syllable her way since they'd left Hope Haven.

"That's not a big deal," Shannon assured him. "A lot of kids have that diagnosis."

That Blake happened to be one of them didn't surprise her, either. She'd been with him only a few hours, and she'd already picked up on his distractibility and fidgetiness. While before she'd been uncomfortable with the idea of her son being placed with another family, she bristled now that some foster parents wouldn't want him. How could they be so cruel as to reject her child?

Blake crossed his arms. "ADHD kids aren't the ones that foster parents are begging to bring home with them. Low on the cute-little-kid scale. Older kids and those who've had trips to juvie are even tougher sales."

Shannon took an unsteady breath as the impact of his words became clear. Blake was a member of all three groups. Three strikes against him in a state system where the statistics weren't on his side. A system she'd subjected him to when she'd signed that voluntary release of parental rights.

"Trooper Shoffner, didn't you say you had good news, too?" She managed to keep her voice level, though she was tempted to beg him to say something offering a little hope.

"Right."

But he waited as if he expected Blake to look over at him. Instead, the boy continued picking at his cuticles, his gaze darting to the side. He was curious, all right. Finally, he sat up and looked at the officer.

"The grocery store owner decided not to press charges. Because of mitigating circumstances, we might be able to have the runaway charges reduced."

Blake's expression remained carefully neutral, the mask of a child who'd learned never to hope for too much. Finally, he nodded. It was something.

Trooper Shoffner didn't take credit for convincing the store owner not to press charges or for speaking to the Oakland County prosecutor, but Shannon suspected he'd done both. She'd practiced adult maneuvering like that when a few of her girls had continued making poor decisions. A fleeting thought reminded her that Hope Haven residents might not wish to be called "her girls" after today, but she couldn't think about that until Blake's situation was under control. And she was beginning to wonder if that was even possible.

Two uniformed officers suddenly filled the doorway. Shannon remembered the muscular male trooper. He was the one who'd taken a report when a boy involved with one of her residents had shown up to cause trouble. She didn't recognize the female trooper, an attractive blonde with her hair tied in a loose bun.

"Now, let me get this right." The man paused, one side of his mouth lifting. "You let a juvenile suspect convince you to take him back to his house, and, instead, he led you to a home for teen mothers? Priceless!"

"Was he hoping to enroll there?" The female trooper laughed at her own joke, and then her gaze narrowed. "Didn't you know about Hope Haven?"

"I do now." Mark gestured toward the other officers. "Trooper Angela Vincent and Trooper Brody Davison, meet Shannon Lyndon and Blake Wilson."

"We've met." Shannon shook Trooper Davison's hand.

He studied her for a few seconds and then nodded. "I remember. A suspect was harassing one of the girls.

A real Dad-of-the-Year. But Trooper Shoffner here will have a better story about his visit to Hope Haven."

Mark frowned as his fellow officer patted him on the back. "Have I mentioned that Mr. Wilson believes Miss Lyndon is his birth mother or that Miss Lyndon does not dispute the claim?"

"What?" Trooper Davison asked.

"Excuse me?" Trooper Vincent chimed.

The officers looked from Mark to Shannon and back to Mark again.

The female officer pressed her hands together. "Clearly we don't have the whole story, so we'll let you get back to it." Already, she started backing away from the door, with the other trooper copying her exit.

"Is there a problem in here?"

Another uniformed officer stood just outside the doorway, blocking their exit in the already cramped space. He had eyeglasses and a boyish face that made him look like a teenager, but from the way the three other officers straightened at his appearance, he was in charge.

"No, Lieutenant." His jaw tightening, Trooper Shoffner shot an annoyed look at his fellow troopers and then gestured to his superior officer. "Everyone, please meet Lt. Matt Dawson."

He made another round of introductions and gestured toward the other troopers. "They were just leaving."

"Uh, he's right," Trooper Davison said. "We have to get back out on patrol."

Lt. Dawson nodded. "I'm sure the residents of Michigan will appreciate your diligence."

Once they had disappeared down the hall, the lieutenant turned back to Mark. "I assume you have this under control, Trooper Shoffner?"

"Yes, sir." But as soon as the officer stepped away, Mark pursed his lips, and his hand thudded on the desktop. "That went well. New guy perks."

Something was going on with Trooper Shoffner at work, but she had more important things than that to worry about right now. Out in the squad room, the state worker was still on her cell phone.

"How do you think she's doing?"

"I'm sure she'll find something soon." Mark looked far less certain than his claim.

"...and thanks so much for your time," the woman said before ending the call.

As the state caseworker reentered the interview room, Shannon held her breath. Something was squeezing her heart from the inside out. She'd felt pain like this only once before. The empty receiving blanket. The void in her arms. She'd just found Blake, and he was being taken away again. Would he be placed far away so she wouldn't have the chance to get to know him? How could she earn his forgiveness if she couldn't be near him?

"I've been making some calls," Miss Lafferty began, "but unfortunately, we've been unable to find a foster placement for Blake this morning—"

"What about an emergency placement?" Mark asked.

"I've tried that, too, but our numbers are really high right now, and with Thanksgiving just days away... Well, even our emergency homes are...unable to house him at this time." As she sat in the only available chair, the woman's gaze shifted to Blake, but then she looked away.

Shannon's pulse thudded in her ears. How dare they turn away her son? But her breath caught as another idea sprang into her thoughts, eclipsing the righteous anger in its wake. Was it possible? Could there be a chance?

She took a deep breath, grasping for calm. "So you're saying that Blake has no place to go?"

The state worker shook her head. "Of course not. There's a spot for him at the Community Children's Center."

"You can't take him there!"

Even Shannon heard the shriek in her voice, so she didn't try to convince herself that the others had missed it. Blake and the trooper shot questioning glances her way. The caseworker stared at her with wide eyes.

"I mean, that's not…er…the most appropriate placement for him."

"It would be a temporary placement, of course," the social worker said with a sigh.

Mark pushed back from the desk, gripping its edge with both hands. "Wait. Community Children's Center is where we incarcerate teens, isn't it?"

Miss Lafferty nodded. "Yes, but it's also an emergency placement location for teens who've been removed from their homes for various reasons."

"You put them together? In the same facility?"

At Mark's incredulous look, the woman blanched. "Well, the boys and girls are kept separate at all times, and—"

"I mean, those serving juvenile sentences and the victims of abuse or neglect," he pressed.

Miss Lafferty opened her mouth as if to offer another explanation, but she clicked it shut. "It's not a perfect solution. But sometimes it's the only option we have to keep the children safe."

"Safe?"

A hard edge had come into the officer's voice, but

Shannon had no time to debate the advisability of placing juvenile offenders with victims of neglect or abuse. Right now she had to protect her own child, the son she'd failed to shield before.

"The center isn't Blake's only option."

The other two adults turned to stare at her.

"Well, it isn't." No longer able to sit, Shannon sprang from her chair and paced toward the door. When she turned back, Miss Lafferty was shaking her head.

"I don't understand what you're saying. Wait." The woman stopped and studied her. "You're not suggesting…"

"Of course I am. I'm Blake's mother…his biological mother. And I am a licensed social worker with a master's in social work, so I could easily receive emergency foster parent certification. I could become his temporary guardian until I—"

"Miss Lyndon," the woman said to interrupt her. "I understand that this has been an emotional day for you and Mr. Wilson, but this…"

Miss Lafferty offered one of those placating smiles that Shannon had used herself with parents enrolling their pregnant teens at Hope Haven. She promised herself never to smile at them that way again.

"You haven't thought this through. You work and live in a center for pregnant girls, not the most appropriate place for an adolescent *boy.*"

"We have a few details to work out, but—"

That annoying smile was enough to stop her. Shannon crossed her arms over her chest.

"You have to know that it isn't as easy as that," Miss Lafferty continued. "There is no proof yet that Mr. Wilson is even your child."

"Of course he's my son. I knew his name was Blake, and he had the letter, and he looks just like—"

She stopped herself and jerked her head to see Blake glaring at her, accusation clear in his eyes. Yes, she had a lot to explain to him about his birth father, among other things, but if she didn't fight right now, she might never have the chance.

"I understand that you're convinced, but the state will need more proof." The woman cleared her throat. "Not to mention the courts."

The last had Shannon tearing her gaze away from her son. "What do you mean by that?"

"Even if we can prove that Mr. Wilson is your biological child, then there's that whole matter of your completing a voluntary release of parental rights. You don't have any—"

"I was fifteen years old!"

"Why do you talk about me as if I'm not sitting right here?" Blake shouted.

He came out of his seat, and although the trooper stood as well and stepped between them to stop the boy if he approached, Mark made no attempt to restrain him. Even he had to realize that Blake had every right to be angry.

Blake pinned the state worker with his stare. "You talk about me like I'm a piece of property."

He pointed at Shannon.

"And you." He paused, his jaw flexing as he gritted his teeth. "You didn't want me then, and you don't really want me now. You just feel guilty because you sent me to live with…them."

Her tears came instantly, and Shannon didn't bother trying to stop them. "No. You're wrong. I always wanted you. They just wouldn't let—"

"I don't want your excuses."

"They're not excuses. Please. Just let me explain."

"I don't want to live with you. I don't want anything to do with you!"

A sob broke loose before Shannon could stop it. The world was crushing her with its unforgiving weight. She'd waited a lifetime to be reunited with Blake. She'd dreamed of it. Prayed for it. Now her chance to even get to know him was slipping away, and there was nothing she could do to stop it. Worse than even the prospect that he would be placed far away from her, if he was sent to the children's center, he might spiral further into delinquency. Would he be lost to her forever?

Miss Lafferty slowly stood. "Many details will have to be taken care of in the coming weeks. For now, I will put in another call to Community Children's Center."

Mark turned to her. "There's another option."

The woman pressed her lips together, losing her patience. "Trooper Shoffner, you called me in to assist here. It's kind of you to be concerned, but this is a complicated situation, and you aren't aware of all of the legalities in it. Now, please allow me to do my job."

"I said, there's another option."

With a long-suffering sigh, the woman met his gaze. "And what might that be?"

"The boy can stay with me."

Chapter Four

What had he done? As Mark allowed the social worker to usher him and Shannon into the hall, he braced his hand on the door frame to steady his head. With six words that had surprised him as much as they had everyone else, he'd done a cannonball dive into a situation that should have been wrapped in crime-scene tape or marked with a sign that said Keep Out. Still, the more he considered his knee-jerk suggestion, the more it seemed like a perfect solution for everyone. Him included.

"What was that all about?" Miss Lafferty said after she closed the door, shutting the interview room off from the squad room. She carried the thick, brown file under her arm like a football.

"Yeah. What were you thinking, saying something like that?" Shannon's eyes were almost as wide as they'd been earlier when Blake had shown up on her doorstep.

"Now, hear me out." But Mark didn't rush to offer a profound explanation. He was figuring that out as he went. Because it was impossible to focus on anything with Shannon looking at him like that, he averted his gaze and spoke directly to the state worker.

"Well…I'm a state trooper." He swallowed. Now,

that was stating the obvious. His gaze slid without his permission toward Shannon, who was shuffling her feet, but he redirected his attention to Miss Lafferty.

"Anyway, I've already been through an extensive background check. I've been fingerprinted, too. An experienced professional like you, Miss Lafferty? You could get someone like me certified as an emergency placement foster parent with both hands tied behind your back."

The woman shook her head, his flattery failing to sway her. Shannon was probably doing the same thing behind him, but he wouldn't allow himself to check. He pressed on, determined to convince them both. He was surprised by how important it had become to him to win the argument.

"Divorced. No dependents. I live alone. I couldn't have less complications for doing something like this."

"Except not having certification," Miss Lafferty pointed out.

"But you can make it happen. You know you can."

Again, she shook her head. "I'm not saying I can't get it approved, Trooper Shoffner. But I have to know. Why do you want to do this?"

Good question. Should he tell her that he was drawn to Blake, who reminded him so much of his former self, from the insolent slouch to that practiced smirk? Or he could admit that by becoming the boy's temporary guardian he could prove once and for all that he'd left his own delinquent past behind. Both excuses were valid, and neither was as bad as confessing that he might have volunteered, at least in part, to play the hero for Blake's desperate mother. That he couldn't bear to admit.

"Haven't the system and the adults in this kid's life

failed him enough already?" So he'd sidestepped the question altogether. That he'd also deflected the attention back to Shannon only confirmed what a coward he was.

This time he couldn't stop himself from glancing at her. She stiffened at his jab, but, to her credit, she continued to look right at him. She didn't even point out that he'd dodged the question better than a politician would on the campaign trail.

"Yes, the boy has had a tough time of it," Miss Lafferty said. "Although I must tell you that some of his foster parents have been good ones."

"Some? But not all?" Shannon searched the other woman's face, as if hoping for assurances that they all knew wouldn't come.

"Most. Not all."

Mark braced his hand on the doorjamb again, this time to hold his frustration in check. The kid deserved better than that. *All kids* deserved better.

"Let's face it. Blake has been bounced around the system for years. He's the real victim in this mess. I don't know about you, but I can't turn my back on him."

"No one is suggesting that we do that," Miss Lafferty said.

"Sorry. That wasn't fair." Mark shook his head, taking hold of his emotions. "What I mean is if we can prevent the system from failing the boy again, then I think we should try. Even if it's only for a while."

Shannon looked back and forth between the police officer and the state worker, her thoughts colliding in a barrage of pipe dreams and practicality, wishes and reality. She still couldn't get over that Trooper Shoffner had offered to give Blake a home. Whether it was a good idea or not, she wasn't sure. This was the same man who'd vacillated between looking at her like a defendant at sentencing and comforting her with words like *You couldn't have known.* Between announcing that she'd failed Blake and offering him a home when she couldn't.

He had offered, though, which was more than most people would have done. Part of her resented his intrusion into their lives. But it was the other part that unnerved her. The one that was tempted to go beyond just being grateful that he'd offered. The one that was tempted to see him as her personal knight in state police blue or something. She couldn't be thinking something like that. She'd learned the hard way never to put her trust in a guy, no matter how desperate she was.

"You don't have a lot of options," Mark said, breaking the silence. "I know *Blake* doesn't."

Shannon swallowed. She couldn't allow this to be about her. It had to be about whatever was best for Blake. The police officer realized it, and he'd known nothing about her son two hours ago. As the person who'd been missing Blake all of his life, how could she have failed to recognize it?

"Thank you," she managed. She didn't care how sour and frightening those words tasted in her mouth. She would do whatever was necessary to help her son.

Miss Lafferty stared at the file in her hands for several seconds and then, as if she'd come to a decision, she looked up and nodded. "So tell me about the experience you've had working with troubled youth, Trooper Shoffner."

"None."

She had her pen poised to write, but she stopped and studied him. "Other children, then? With those of which ages have you had the most experience?"

"Look. This will go faster if I tell you that I haven't worked with children. But I can figure it out."

"None?" Shannon couldn't keep the squeak out of her voice. "Ever?" Before, she'd been annoyed by his meddling, and now she was worried that he wouldn't get the chance.

Miss Lafferty lifted a brow. "You've got to be—"

"I may not have experience working with kids," Mark said to interrupt her, "but I can relate to the boy in that room better than either of you can."

The state social worker lifted her chin and stared at him. "How is that?"

Mark bent his head, blowing out a breath. "I was just like him."

"What do you mean?" Miss Lafferty asked. "A foster kid? An angry teen with a juvenile record?"

"A runaway?" Shannon couldn't help adding.

"All of the above…except for the foster kid part." At their questioning gazes, Mark held his hands wide. "Every family needs a black sheep. I was ours."

Although he chuckled as he said it, the shadow that passed over his face gave Shannon a glimpse at the pain behind his words. Something tightened inside her belly. She was painfully aware of how a person's past could follow him, but she couldn't let herself wonder how the trooper's history played upon his present. She had enough trouble in her own life without prying into his.

"Still, I worry that your lack of experience with troubled teens would make this too hard on you," Miss Lafferty said.

"I have that."

Only when the other adults turned to her did Shannon realize she'd said those words aloud.

"Well, it's true. I have plenty of experience with troubled teens. I could help him out. Offer some tips."

But Mark was already shaking his head. "Thanks. But I can handle it."

"Really. I can help. I have about twelve girls at Hope Haven at any given time."

"I'll be fine. Thanks."

She crossed her arms. "I doubt that."

His jaw tightened, and he stared at her until she looked away. "You've known Blake for two hours, and now you're an expert on him?"

"I never said that. I only said I know about troubled kids." Shannon pressed her lips together to prevent herself from saying more, but this time she couldn't stop the words from coming. "You can judge me all you want. Even without the whole story. But know this. I have loved my son every minute of every hour of his life, whether he was with me or not." Though her eyes burned, she refused to cry again. "I had planned to find him when he turned eighteen. Whether he realizes it or not, he needs me."

"You're right about that."

At the intrusion of Miss Lafferty's voice, Shannon regretted that she'd lashed out, but she still couldn't help wondering how the officer would have answered if given a chance. Why did she care? Why had she allowed him to get under her skin?

"Blake's going to need you both." Miss Lafferty waved away their arguments. "Neither of you can handle this alone. But together… Well, it just might work."

Shannon met Mark's wary gaze with her own cautious one, worrying now that working with him would be a bad idea.

"You." The state worker pointed at Shannon. "Whatever you were planning to do when you met him in four years no longer matters. Blake is here now, although as yet we haven't proved he's your son. Even after that, it's going to be a long, tough road before you can reestablish a legal connection to him. You'll need a lot of help—including mine—to make that happen."

Shannon drew her brows together in confusion, but Miss Lafferty must have been satisfied she'd made her point because she dismissed her.

"And you, Trooper. You've offered to take in this boy, but you have zero experience working with kids like him, except for yourself. That doesn't really count. I can help you receive emergency certification, if you pass the home visit, but you'll need additional help while you're catching up with the training hours." She indicated Shannon with a wave of her arm. "She knows how to handle kids like Blake, and she's willing to share some of the lessons she's learned with you."

When he shook his head, Miss Lafferty nodded hers.

"I realize you didn't have time to really think about this before you volunteered, but did you consider that your job won't allow you to be home 24/7, though Blake needs regular supervision?" She crossed her arms. "Didn't think so."

Mark opened his mouth as if to respond, but then he closed it again.

"In addition to welcoming her suggestions, I recommend that you hire Miss Lyndon to stay with Blake when you're working and he's out of school."

Shannon held her breath as the possibility dangled there before her, almost within reach. A regular schedule with Blake. Time to love him. Time to explain. She was so caught up in the prospect that she didn't realize at first that the room had become quiet. The others were watching her, waiting.

"Sorry. What were you saying?"

"I wanted to know if your work schedule is flexible enough for you to help Trooper Shoffner out."

"Oh. Sure. I'll just switch shifts with Katie, the other social worker." She shot a glance at Mark, but he pointedly looked away from her. "I won't take any pay for it, though."

"Then it's settled," Miss Lafferty said with a nod.

Mark said nothing. He stood with his legs in a wide stance and his arms crossed, an intimidating posture that probably had criminals laying their weapons at his feet.

Miss Lafferty pursed her lips. "Bottom line. Either you agree to work together for Blake's sake, or I will be forced to recommend placing him at the children's center."

Mark cleared his throat. "Fine by me."

Shannon could only nod. Was there really a chance that all of this could work out?

"Great. Trooper Shoffner, you'll provide a temporary home for Blake until Miss Lyndon's maternity can be established and legal matters are settled. And Miss Lyndon, you'll provide after-school supervision and parenting support." She held her hands wide and smiled as if she'd just solved all the world's problems. "That will work out fine…at least until a more permanent placement is located."

Shannon's breath caught. Of course it was only temporary. She knew that. So why did this interim plan seem so incredibly brief now?

But Trooper Shoffner and Miss Lafferty had moved past the subject, as if it wasn't worth even a pause. Mark had made some suggestion about Blake doing community service with him before his juvenile court date to encourage the judge's leniency, and the state worker agreed it was a good idea.

"We should do it right on Hope Haven's grounds." Mark's gaze darted to Shannon. "The place looks like it could use some work. Cracked gutters. Ripped screens. Broken concrete."

Shannon's cheeks burned. "Well, money's tight right now. Nonprofits, you know. There's not even room in the budget for repair supplies. I appreciate the offer, but—"

"I'll get donations for that," Mark said, as if fundraising wasn't a constant challenge for charitable organizations.

With some of the details in place, they returned to the interview room, where Blake slouched low as though it didn't matter to him what had happened outside that door. And what was about to happen with his life. Shannon didn't buy his indifference any more than the others should have accepted her own mask of certainty. Now shell-shocked, that was exactly what she was.

As if providing a home for Blake wasn't enough, Trooper Shoffner had volunteered not only to do repairs on the Hope Haven buildings that were falling down around them but also to find a way to pay for improvements.

Still, she couldn't worry now about her lingering doubts over all the plans they'd made, or even the recurring image of Mark as that knight in the blue squad car with its red spinning light. None of that was important. Not now that Shannon and a ticking clock had been drafted to opposing teams. Mounting a legal custody challenge and building a solid mother-son relationship with a child who wanted nothing to do with her would be challenging enough without adding the pressure of a looming deadline. She had no choice, though, but to tackle both of those monumental tasks before Blake could be placed in another foster home. Possibly somewhere far away.

Seconds ticked on a loudspeaker in her ears. This tiny window of time might be her only opportunity to get to know Blake, to earn his forgiveness. Would he give her the chance? He had to. And she had to make this right with him, had to show him that no matter how wrong her decisions had been, she'd made them out of love. She had to do it…before time ran out.

"So why'd you do it?"

At Blake's question, Mark looked up from the kitchen sink where he'd just put the pans in the sudsy water. He didn't look back at him, but he didn't pretend to miss the boy's meaning, either. This was the most civil comment Blake had made all night. The twelve hours of foster parent training the private agency would still require Mark to take would be nothing compared to these three hours of introduction by fire.

Mark took his time drying his hands on a towel. "It was the right thing to do."

"For me, you or my *mother?*"

He swallowed, and this time he glanced over his shoulder at the boy. Leaning against the kitchen doorway, his arms and ankles crossed, Blake stared right at him. What did the kid know? Had he noticed that Mark hadn't been able to resist looking at Shannon's smooth-looking skin, at her full, kissable lips? Had *she* noticed?

"For everyone," he somehow managed.

He hoped the finality in his words would put an end

to that line of questioning. He tried not to dwell on the way Blake had stressed the word *mother,* nor on how succinctly he'd encapsulated the situation. And Mark's uncertainties. Out of the mouths of surly teens....

"Nobody asked me what I wanted."

"Guess not."

Mark wasn't about to ask him now, either. Instead, he dunked his hands in the soapy water and tackled the pan with pasta noodles stuck to the bottom. All night Blake had made it clear that Mark's three-bedroom rental home was the last place he wanted to be. He'd complained about everything from their dinner of slightly charred hamburgers and boxed macaroni to the bare walls and the basic bed and dresser in the guest room. And if Mark had ever been under the mistaken impression that Blake thought the plan to work at Hope Haven tomorrow was a good idea, then the kid had set him straight about that.

Okay, Blake had a point about the dinner. It hadn't been Mark's most shining culinary moment. But he'd been wrong to call the freshly painted two-story a dump. At least it had the bedroom and bathroom locks required for the foster care home visit.

Shutting off the water, Mark glanced over his shoulder again, but Blake was gone, so the opportunity had passed. He probably should have laid down some rules such as that the boy would help him clean up after meals. He should have done many things. Too bad for him he didn't know what they were.

What had he been thinking, volunteering to become a foster parent? And, worse yet, offering to do work at Hope Haven. He was in so far over his head that his hands wouldn't break the surface if he held them straight up and started jumping up and down. Just because seeing Blake was like looking at his fourteen-year-old self in the mirror, it didn't mean that at thirty-three he had any idea what to do with the kid.

The disappointment-filled voices of his parents, of his brothers, of his ex-wife, Kim, even, the same ones that had been whispering in the background all day as he'd arranged details for Blake's arrival, boomed in his ears now. The wheelchair-bound image of Chris Lawson stared back at him, a permanent reminder of the mistakes that Mark couldn't take back. If he'd thought that working with one troubled teenager would be enough to prove that he was no longer the guy in that accident, then he'd never considered what would happen if his charity project was a major failure. And right now it looked as if that was exactly what it would be.

When the floor creaked behind him, Mark blinked away the painful memories and turned to find Blake standing there with a stack of plates, cups and silverware in his hands. Mark accepted the stack with a nod of thanks, and then as he returned to the sink, the boy spoke from behind him.

"But *you* didn't have to do it."

"Guess not," he said again, though this time he had to forcibly keep his voice calm.

He could just imagine Blake staring at his back, trying to understand the angle he was playing with his offer of help. At least the boy, who was more accustomed to people failing to meet their obligations than those volunteering out of true charity, wouldn't be surprised by Mark's self-serving purpose. That only made Mark feel guiltier over Blake's comment, which was the closest thing the boy would give to a thank-you. His chest squeezed with something unfamiliar and a little scary. He was becoming attached, which might have been his biggest mistake of all.

Once the last dish was in the dishwasher, he started in the direction that Blake had taken. He found him in the living room, watching television. Blake patted the spot next to him on the navy corduroy sofa and then gestured toward the brown-and-orange-plaid recliner near the window.

"Your ex must have really taken you to the cleaners."

His jaw tightened, but he forced himself to remain calm. The boy was baiting him, maybe to step back from the words he'd said before. No matter how much Mark wanted to declare that subject off-limits, he wouldn't give the kid the satisfaction of knowing he'd gotten to him.

"Yeah, we get a raw deal in life sometimes," he said instead. "But I guess you already know about that."

Blake shrugged, sank back into the sofa that Mark had intended to be only a temporary furnishing and started flipping through the channels.

Mark smiled. He'd asked himself how he could dive into this mess of a situation, but he hadn't asked the more important question: How could he not? It was the right thing to do for Blake's sake—the Christian thing to do. With everything Blake had faced in his young life, he deserved to have someone unapologetically in his court.

Blake also deserved the chance to get to know his probable birth mother, even if Mark was taking a risk by exposing the boy again to a woman who'd once given away her own child. Mark hoped that Shannon was ready to commit to her son now, to be the mother he deserved, but if she still couldn't do it, at least he could be there to support the boy. Although he might not be able to protect Blake completely, at least he could shield him from some of the pain.

Chapter Five

Shannon's breath caught as a silver extended-cab pickup drove past the kitchen window, spitting gravel until it came to a stop in front of the pole barn. Not that seeing it should have surprised her when she'd been cleaning the sink long enough for it to have a showroom shine while waiting for Mark and Blake to arrive.

At least with the two of them on the Hope Haven grounds, it wouldn't be so quiet there. The place had been tomblike ever since she'd returned home yesterday afternoon and the girls had started in with their silent treatment. Fair or unfair, the silence magnified every squeak of the old floorboards, every click of a door latch, and it was making her climb out of her skin.

Now she tried to convince herself that it was *only* the prospect of seeing her son that had her face feeling flushed because it couldn't have anything to do with the man driving the truck. But when the driver's door opened, a work-booted foot stepped out onto the running board and a muscular, jeans-clad calf came into view, she stuck her hands under the running water. If her palms were a little sweaty, at least she didn't have to admit it this way.

What was the matter with her? Hadn't she ever seen a man in scuffed work boots before? Trying not to rush, she dried off her hands, pulled on a fleece jacket and came down the back steps, crossing the drive to the barn. It was as cold as it had been yesterday when Blake had stood on her front porch in that flimsy zip up, but at least it wasn't as windy.

When Shannon reached the truck, Mark had closed the door and was shrugging into a heavy work jacket. He wasn't wearing his uniform this time, but instead of having the decency to look like a slob, he had the gall to look just as great in faded jeans and a thread-bare red-plaid shirt.

She was just considering how a leather tool belt might perfectly accent Mark's construction-worker ensemble when Blake stepped around the bed of the truck. If she'd ever needed a reminder of why they were all there together—the only reason—he was standing right in front of her. Why did she keep losing track of her priorities whenever the police officer was around?

"Blake, I'm so glad you're here."

He didn't answer, instead finding something interesting on the ground to study. With the toe of his scuffed work boot, he shifted the broken piece of cement. She wanted to tell him how handsome he looked now that his still-messy hair was at least clean and he'd shaved the crop of hairs on his chin, but she doubted that he would appreciate the compliment. He was determined to hate her. How was she ever going to build a relationship with him if he didn't give her a chance?

"New clothes?" She indicated the weathered jeans and hoodie sweatshirt that hung on his thin frame. At least they were clean. Over them he wore a newer-looking winter jacket.

Blake's nose wrinkled with distaste. "They're his."

The crunch of gravel announced the officer's approach, but she didn't need the sound to know that Mark was just behind her. The odd awareness she had around him was really starting to bug her.

"We figured he shouldn't ruin the new stuff on the first day," Mark said.

She turned to the side. "Oh. Hi, Trooper Shoffner." She managed not to wince. Was she trying to convince him that she hadn't noticed he was there?

He shook his head. "Nope. Not on the job right now, so it's just Mark."

"Okay…Mark." She tested the name on her tongue. It felt a little too informal for the distance she planned to keep between them, but how could she tell him that without explaining why she needed that distance? "This…uh…*is* my work, but you can still call me Shannon."

He nodded but didn't try it out, which was just as well. She would probably like the way he said it. Maybe she should have kept it at Miss Lyndon after all.

"And we all know I'm Blake," the boy nearly spat. "So are we going to get started or what?"

Her cheeks burned. Could even Blake see how flustered she became around the police officer?

"Yeah. Of course. So…um…Mark, where would you want to get started?"

"Anywhere is probably good," Blake answered before he could and then gave Mark a conspiratorial grin. "This place is almost as much of a dump as yours is."

"Yeah." The side of Mark's mouth lifted. "But it makes my house look like a palace."

"It would be a better idea to level the joint and start over."

Great. They were going to talk *around* her just like her girls had been doing all morning. Could one person here at least pretend to commiserate with her over the awkward situation she was in now?

"Yes, I realize there are several projects that need attention." She couldn't keep her chin from lifting as she said it. This was her life's work after all, and they were making fun of it. "The churches in the ecumenical council support Hope Haven, but with the recession, all of their offering plates have been lighter than normal."

"Hey. Sorry," Mark said. "I just—"

She cleared her throat to interrupt him and then licked her lips as shame welled. If she was a better fund-raiser, then maybe they wouldn't be in this situation. "As I mentioned, there isn't a budget for significant repairs. Or any, really."

But Mark wasn't listening. He kept several steps ahead, scanning the edge of the roof at the back of the house, his gaze following the line of the gutters to the downspouts at the foundation.

"You have leaks in the basement, don't you?"

"A few." She frowned. "Wait. You can tell that by looking out here?"

"These downspouts are too short. They should have extenders so they come out farther from the foundation. The gutters have probably been blocked up there for years, too." He pointed to a spot in the gutter with peeling paint and an obvious crack. "In an old place like this, there could be several reasons why the basement's leaking, but we should try to fix the ones we can."

"That's great, but as I said—"

He didn't even look back at her. "I told you I would take care of the financing."

"But how?" She should have asked that question yesterday, but she'd been too worried about what would happen with Blake to have paid close attention to the other matters they'd discussed.

"The troopers at the Brighton Post have agreed to make Hope Haven a pet charity project for the next few months. We're raising some money through our friends and families, and then several of the troopers have offered to help with the work."

"You did all of that since yesterday in addition to enrolling Blake in his new school and buying him new clothes?"

Mark shot a look at Blake, who'd pulled the hood up around his ears and was staring up at the gutters. "When else was I supposed to do those things?"

He made it sound simple, but Mark had done plenty of things in the past twenty-four hours, beyond putting the fund-raising directors from local nonprofits to shame. She was relieved he didn't enumerate all of the tasks he'd had to accomplish to bring Blake into his home. Feeling indebted to him was hard enough without having him list the details in a balance sheet where she was deeply in the red.

As if he was uncomfortable with making a big deal about his accomplishments since yesterday, Mark returned to his pickup and unlocked the silver toolbox that stretched across the truck bed. Dozens of hand tools and several power tools, their cords wrapped in tidy figure eights, were stored inside.

"When is he supposed to start at school?" she asked as he took inventory of his equipment.

"Not until the Monday after Thanksgiving. Since next week is only a three-day week, the counselor thought it would be better for me to help him get settled first." He was winding another perfect cord on a power drill, but suddenly he turned back to her. "Wait. You didn't say whether you were able to make an appointment with the family law attorney."

She watched Blake for a few seconds as he stared up at the roof. "Yes, on Monday, but the attorney already gave me a preview of what I'm up against. I understand now what Miss Lafferty meant when she said that I would need her."

"What do you mean?"

"Apparently, as a birth parent who signed a voluntary release of parental rights, I am not one of the parties who can legally request a court modification of a permanent custody order."

"And all of that means…?"

"That I would need the state agency to request the change in the custody order because I can't. It's going to be an uphill battle." She paused and lifted her chin. "But hills don't scare me."

Mark studied her for several seconds, but then he glanced over at the truck as if he'd forgotten something. "What about the DNA test? Don't you have to start there?"

"We'll want to get that done as soon as possible. We can go to the hospital lab on Monday to have a buccal swab taken for a chain of custody DNA test. It's the only kind of test that's admissible in court."

"That's just a swab that collects cells from the inside of your cheek, right?" He waited for her nod before he continued. "How long before you know if Blake is your kid?"

"Well, I already know, but I have to wait five to seven business days for medical proof."

At that, he nodded, but he didn't say whether or not

he believed she was Blake's birth mother. He returned his attention to the tools in his case.

"Hey, Blake. A little help over here?"

But the boy still stood in that same spot behind the house. He pointed to the roof. "You're out of your mind if you think I'm going up there."

Mark chuckled, the sound low and deep. "If you think I'd trust you up there, then you've got another *think* coming. You'll be holding the ladder."

"Sure you want to trust me to do that? One slip and…" Blake moved his hand in a circular motion to indicate the fall Mark might take.

Mark gave him a mean look and turned back to Shannon. "Now, if you can lead us to the ladder, then you'll be free to head back inside while we get started."

Had she just been dismissed? "Don't you need me to—"

"No. We'll be fine."

Her mouth seemed to have fallen open of its own accord, so she clicked it closed. Why had Mark even suggested that he and Blake work at Hope Haven if he only planned to keep her son away from her? She'd been duped. He'd probably agreed to partner with her only to keep Blake from having to go to the children's center, not to help her get to know her son. Would he go back on his word to let her supervise Blake while he was at work? Come to think of it, he'd dodged the question about why he'd volunteered in the first place. If she'd called him on it at the time, then she wouldn't be in this position now.

It wasn't fair. He was acting as a gatekeeper to her son. Wasn't it enough that her parents had practically forced her to give away her child? Now Mark was playing games with her by making it possible for her to be near Blake and yet putting himself between them so they couldn't get too close. Why was he doing that? But more important than that, how could she make him stop?

"So…the ladder?"

She indicated the barn with a flip of her thumb. "There are a few things out there. Ladder. Wheelbarrow. Maybe a hammer or two."

"Good. Thanks." He took a few steps toward the barn and then turned back.

She followed the line of his gaze to where Blake had remained near the house. No longer alone, the boy stood staring at the five girls across from him. Their curiosity appeared mutual.

Brooke stepped forward first, her mess of dark brown curls flying in her face. At almost seventeen, she was the most senior Hope Haven resident in both age and in weeks of her pregnancy.

"Hi, I'm Brooke."

She reached out a hand to Blake. He stood motionless for a few heartbeats, his gaze locked on the fullness of her abdomen that peeked out from her fleece jacket, but then he must have caught himself staring because he stepped forward and shook her hand. "I'm… um…Blake."

Shannon pressed her lips together, trying not to smile at his stammering. She mourned the years she'd been absent from his childhood, but this was a reminder that she hadn't missed it all. He was still young enough to be shy around girls.

Since the oldest resident had introduced herself, it only seemed right that the youngest stepped forward next. "Hey, I'm Chelsea."

Rolling his lips inward, Blake nodded at her.

With heavy limbs, Shannon crossed the yard to the group. The reception to her from both sides was frostier than the outside air.

"Girls, I didn't get the chance to introduce you all yesterday." She paused, taking in a breath so deep her lungs ached, and then exhaled slowly. "But I would like to you to meet Blake. My son."

The girls' gazes flicked her way, but almost as one, they looked away from her. She'd hurt them, all right, just as she'd hurt Blake.

"I gave up a baby for adoption when I was fifteen." She paused, her gaze lingering on Chelsea, the only one of them who, like Shannon, would experience motherhood before she could drive. "We still have to have proof for the state that we're biologically related, but I don't need proof. He's my son."

She might have just imagined the stark vulnerability in Blake's eyes because it was there one second and gone the next. He pointedly looked away from her.

Denise made a big show of studying Shannon's face and then repeated the exercise on Blake. "He looks like you," she said finally. "Especially the eyes."

Shannon cleared her throat. "I should have told you all about this before. That I knew what you were going through. That I understood."

"We can talk about that later." Chelsea indicated Blake with a shift of her head.

Shannon nodded.

"It's okay, Miss Shannon," Brooke told her.

But it wasn't. None of them would ever understand why she'd kept her secret. She nodded her thanks anyway, trying her best to smile. "And, Blake, I'd like you to meet Sam, Denise and Jacqui."

As they exchanged hellos, Blake did a good job of

keeping eye contact with them rather than staring at their stomachs. If Shannon's smile had been forced before, it was authentic now. He must have understood how much her girls hated people staring at them when they were out in public. She couldn't take credit for her son's good manners, however, as she'd played no role in his developing those. But she was glad that somewhere along the way someone had taught them to him.

Mark had been standing back, watching the introductions, but now he called over to them. "Hey, Blake, can you give me a hand with the ladder? Nobody's paying us the big bucks to stand around. We need to get something done while the weather's still holding out."

For the first time, Shannon noticed the ominous clouds that this time of year could signal snow as easily as rain. "Okay, girls, let's let them get to work. We have a list of our own chores inside."

"Aw, man," came the collective response.

"Do we have to?" Sam asked.

"The sooner we get started, the sooner we'll be finished and you can download more library books on your ereader," Shannon told her.

That must have been good enough for Sam because the group's resident bookworm waved and headed off into the house. With only minor grumbling, the other four followed. They'd all had what they considered valid reasons to be angry with Shannon, and yet it appeared the girls were willing to forgive her.

If only it were as easy with Blake and with his new foster dad. Both were treating her like a convict on early release, no longer contained within cramped cell walls or trapped inside an electric fence, but still held by the ankle monitor that kept her from true freedom. Blake had searched for her and yet he'd announced that he wanted nothing to do with her. Mark had almost single-handedly provided her with the opportunity to get to know her son and now seemed to be planting himself as a roadblock to that opportunity.

What could she do? She'd already allowed others to pressure her into missing so many years of Blake's life. She couldn't let that happen again. She would find a way to reach Blake, with or without Mark's help. Nobody was going to stop her.

The storm-heavy clouds made good on their threat by late morning. No matter how much Mark wanted to keep space between him and Blake and the ladies of Hope Haven, it wasn't worth getting a lightning zap to stay on that rickety old ladder.

By the time that he and Blake had stuffed the ladder and the wheelbarrow full of leaves back in the barn, their coats were soaked, and they were shivering.

"This way." Mark waved his arm and took off at a run toward the back of the house.

Blake caught up with him as he opened the storm door. "Wow, staying with you is better than staying on the streets. Drier, too."

"You're not a cube of sugar." Mark let the boy inside on the doormat and then leaned out the open door to shake out his hair. "You won't melt."

"Sure about that?" Blake leaned out and shook his head as well and then pulled the door closed.

Shannon appeared in the doorway then, a stack of towels in her arms stretching up to her chin. "Sorry, guys. You must be freezing. I should have insisted that you come inside before the storm hit."

"It's just rain. We won't melt," Blake grumbled as he accepted a pair of towels and started rubbing his head.

Catching the towels as Shannon tossed them, Mark hid his grin. The kid had a quandary, all right, choosing between playing the tough guy and accepting some loving care from the pretty lady. Right now, the thug was ahead, but Blake wouldn't be able to hold out for long with Shannon trying so hard to win him over. Mark sure wouldn't have been able to resist if she was working that hard to get *his* attention.

He closed his eyes, wiping his face with the towel extra hard to clear his head. He had to stop thinking things like that. Shannon Lyndon hadn't done a thing to encourage his attention, and he was noticing her, anyway. What was wrong with him? Since the divorce, he'd been as gun-shy as any guy who carried a gun for a living could be. And he'd been smart to be cautious after the scars that Kim had left behind by deserting him and their wedding vows. So what was he thinking taking a second glance at someone like Shannon, someone with a track record of deserting her own son?

After pulling off his sopping coat and resting it next to the back door, he glanced out the window where the skies continued to bluster and weep. His relief over having the chance to leave Hope Haven now shamed him. Coming here had been his idea in the first place, though Shannon hadn't exactly painted signs in protest. She'd recognized it as a way to have more time with her son, and she'd climbed on board.

So now that he'd figured out that spending this much time at Hope Haven with the center's pretty housemother might be as big a mistake as throwing himself into Blake's life in the first place, he was stuck. Every time this morning that Shannon had found some flimsy excuse to come outside and say something to Blake,

Mark had been so distracted that he'd nearly fallen off the ladder. It was a mistake, all right, and a health risk.

"We won't be getting any more work done today, so…"

Still holding a few dry towels, Shannon was watching Blake shed his coat, but she looked over at the sound of Mark's words.

"Oh…you don't have to go, do you? I'm sure you could find some things to do inside."

Blake pointed to the door. "I thought we were leaving now."

Mark nodded. "Well, I—"

"I mean," she began, trampling his words, "I fix the things I can, but my home-repair skills are sadly limited. The garbage disposal shoots food everywhere, one of the washing machines leaks all over the floor every time we use it and the upstairs toilet keeps overflowing."

"Sounds like a mess, literally and figuratively," he said, waggling his brows. "How did it get to this point?"

Apparently she didn't like his question because she lifted her chin. "We're doing the best we can. We try not to charge more than our residents' parents can afford to pay, and after we've provided for healthy food, prenatal vitamins, online curriculum, school supplies and small salaries for the staff, there's not a lot left over for minor repairs. We call those things our little inconveniences."

"Sorry." As obvious as it was that Shannon loved the center, Mark could only imagine what it had cost her to confess the facility's deficiencies. The kind of shortcomings that could hurt her during a health department inspection.

"Well, we wouldn't want you to get written up for any of those things, so…"

"So we won't be leaving," Blake finished for him.

Mark thought for a few seconds, the coward in him arm wrestling with the hero wannabe. Losing. "Guess not."

The coward couldn't resist requesting a rematch though. "But won't the place be cramped with everyone inside doing their chores?"

Shannon was already at the door, hefting the heavy coats off the floor. "That shouldn't be a problem," she said over her shoulder. "I'll ask the girls to work in other parts of the house."

But where would *she* be? That was what concerned him most. Either she'd missed the point in his question, or she'd refused to hear it. Didn't she understand that he'd had a difficult enough time working with her inside and him and Blake outside? Now he would have to try to accomplish something, knowing that she was just a room or two away, able to pop in any old time she wanted.

"I'll throw these into one of the dryers so you'll have them for later." She indicated the coats in her arms.

"The dryers work?" Mark couldn't help asking.

She frowned. "For now, anyway."

"Well, we'd better move fast, before they go on the blink, too."

She smiled this time, and he couldn't help wondering if those lips would feel as soft as they looked when pressed to his. He brushed at his eyes to blur the image, but it remained startlingly clear. As much as he wanted to apply his blinders with her, something about her kept pulling them aside and giving him a good look. He didn't want to linger on her china-doll face or to wonder if her shiny ponytail would be soft to touch, but he couldn't stop himself.

She either hadn't noticed him staring or was taking pity on him and giving him a release from his humiliating trance because she opened the basement door and headed down the stairs to the laundry room. Again, he glanced out the window to a sky as cloudy as his thoughts. Why was he allowing a woman to distract him from his goal of proving himself through his work with the troubled teenager? He'd made the mistake once of seeking the thrill of the moment while losing sight of what was important, and that had ended in a mass of tangled metal. If he wasn't careful, all he might prove with this project was that he hadn't changed at all.

Chapter Six

"Have any of you ever been in a situation where you questioned God's purpose in it, or if He even had one?"

Reverend Bill Hicks deadpanned the question to the all-female congregation, and snickers began in the back of the makeshift sanctuary in Hope Haven's formal parlor. They spread faster than a rumor. Shannon couldn't help chuckling along with them, no matter how uncomfortable the thought made her. If God saw some purpose in the awful things that had happened to Blake, or in what her parents had forced her to do, then it had escaped her.

Reverend Hicks was the last to join in with them, his chuckle friendly and warm. Of the visiting ministers who rotated weeks in conducting services at the center, the kind grandfather was Shannon's favorite. He didn't feel compelled to browbeat the girls about their pregnancies the way some of the other ministers did. What point was there for them to schedule special church services for the girls so they could avoid judgmental stares if the ministers only brought more judgments into the house with them?

"Yes, I figured you all just might be able to relate

to that." He chuckled again, and then his expression became solemn. "But I'm telling you now that our Father has a purpose in all things. Even in our most difficult times."

His expression turned serious as he stood at the lectern that faced the wingback chairs and settees serving as pews. "In Romans 8:28, Paul tells us that '…in everything God works for good with those who love Him.'"

Several of the girls shifted in their seats, suggesting that the sermon had either gone on too long for the pressure on their bladders or that they weren't convinced of God's purpose in their dark days. Tonya twisted her hair around her index finger, staring through the filmy lace curtains to the outside. Shannon could second the girl's vote to be somewhere else, but she had a more specific destination in mind. In a few hours, she would be spending time with Blake—just the two of them—while Mark worked a last two-to-ten shift before the time off he'd scheduled to help the boy get settled.

"Oh, I see you questioning." The reverend smiled as he drew in their attention again. "I probably would, too, if I was taking time out from my regular life, like you, and waiting to hatch like an egg under a heat lamp. Just remember to trust in God. You might not see immediately how He can use a difficult situation, but His purpose may become clearer to you down the road."

The minister closed the service in prayer then, but his last words repeated in her mind. Was this her *down the road?* Maybe God had used those awful times in Blake's past to bring them to the point where they could be together. Yes, it was beginning to make sense to her. She'd been looking forward to her time with Blake all morning, but now she couldn't wait to get there. While before everything had seemed so complicated, it was suddenly simple. Now all she had to do was to get Blake on board, and everything would be perfect.

"No, I'm *still* not hungry," Blake called from inside the bedroom where he'd been holed up behind a locked door for hours. "I don't want to talk. I don't want to watch TV. And I don't want to have a mother-son video game tournament either, in case you're interested."

The hand that Shannon had raised to knock on the door again fell limply to her side. What more could she do? She'd thought that the smell of the food she'd prepared for the late-night meal he'd said he didn't want would eventually draw him out. He was a teenage boy after all. One who'd recently missed a few meals at that. Now the truth became clear—Blake would rather starve than spend a single minute alone with her.

"I will not cry."

But even as she whispered the declaration, the tears came hot and wet. She hated crying, and that was all she'd been doing since meeting her son on Friday. Some expert she was in working with troubled youth when she couldn't make any headway with her own son. Again, she was struck with the stark possibility that Blake wouldn't give her the chance to know him. How could she bear it if he didn't? He was so close that she could almost hear his breathing, and yet he couldn't have been further away from her. Out of her arms again. This time by choice.

Defeated, she descended the stairs and returned to the kitchen nook where the food she'd prepared was growing cold on the plates. Now the thought of the table she'd set for two seemed more than optimistic. Downright dumb was closer to it.

She didn't bother sitting at the table, where she'd

arranged sautéed chicken, rice and green beans on the plates. Instead, she dished the food into a few of the mismatched plastic containers she'd found in one of the cabinets and stored them in the refrigerator. Just as she'd toweled off the last pan and was putting it in the cabinet, two headlights flashed on the window.

Only a few minutes later, Mark turned a key in the back door lock but only edged the door open. "Is it safe to come in?"

"You mean, am I armed?"

He pushed the door the rest of the way open. He was in the same street clothes he'd been wearing when he'd left for his shift that afternoon, and he carried the same case that probably contained his weapon.

"Never hurts to be cautious."

"Busy day at work?"

She could do this. She could pretend that everything was fine, that she hadn't spent the past eight hours fighting for the only thing she'd ever wanted. Losing by many steps, big and small.

"Pretty routine, really." But then Mark stopped, tilted his head and watched her for several seconds. "Tell me what happened."

Shannon brushed at her face, though the tears had long since dried. Could he tell she'd been crying? She considered putting him off, but his eyes were so full of concern that she couldn't keep her shoulders from slumping. "Blake's been sulking in his room all night. He won't…come out."

She hated that her voice hitched when she said the last, but she couldn't keep herself from adding, "He's never going to give me a chance."

"You've got that all figured out from one night?"

Shannon blinked. They weren't the compassionate

words she'd hoped for, but she shouldn't have expected them from a guy who'd never bothered to hide his disapproval of her. "I don't expect you to understand."

"Oh, I understand."

This time she just stared at him.

Mark took his time shrugging off his coat and hanging it on a peg on the wall. "I couldn't get him to come out at first the other night, either."

"At first? That means he did come out eventually."

His lips lifted. "Yes, but he doesn't have as much to be mad with me about."

She swallowed, the comment like a kick when she was already down. "Wait. You *arrested* him."

"Good point." Rather than say more, he leaned casually against the wall, waiting.

"I tried everything. Talking to him through the door. Issuing several invitations. Cooking even though he refused to eat so that he would smell the food and get hungry."

"Remind me to steer clear of you when you want to get your way. You pull out all the stops."

She smiled at that. "I even played loud music on your stereo in the most offensive-to-teens genre I could think of to make him want to come out and shut it off."

He lifted a brow. "What was that?"

"The music? Classical."

"Good choice."

"He didn't even comment on it. He just stayed there." Tears welled in her eyes again. "I even considered smoking him out."

"Well, thanks for thinking twice on that one. It's hard enough being the new guy at the post. I would never have lived it down if you set my house on fire while I was at work."

"I had all of these great plans for tonight. I thought I knew everything about troubled teens, too." She stared at her hands. "I don't know what I expected."

As much as Mark tried to resist their impact, Shannon's slumped shoulders, her blotchy skin and swollen eyes from earlier tears tugged at his heart. For Blake's sake he'd wanted to be indifferent to her, but he wondered if that was in Blake's best interest at all. Maybe he should try to convince the boy to give her a chance to prove herself. He knew he would have given anything for the opportunity to prove himself to his parents… before it was too late.

"Maybe you expected too much too soon," he said in a soft voice.

"But I'm running out of time."

His chest squeezed over the anguish in her voice, and he had to hold his hands to his sides to keep from reaching out to her. He didn't know whether it was her words or the twin tears that traced down her cheeks, but he'd lost the battle to remain immune to her pain. Instead of her defiant announcement that she wasn't afraid of a tough legal battle, it was her broken spirit tonight that convinced him of her sincerity. She was as determined to be a mother to her son as he was to draw a line in indelible marker between the boy he'd been and the man he'd become. He had to respect her determination.

Instead of answering, he took the teakettle off the rear burner of the stove and filled it in the sink.

"Orange pekoe or Earl Grey?"

"Oh, that's okay." But when he looked back at her from the stove, she shrugged. "Earl Grey."

He pointed to the dinette she'd cleared earlier, indicating for her to take a seat. She sat but immediately popped up again.

"If you're hungry, I put the leftovers, a whole dinner, really, in the refrigerator."

"Sit, will you? I already ate, and it doesn't look like you're going to, so why waste it?"

She shrugged and dropped back into the seat. Neither of them spoke until the teakettle whistled and Mark poured the water, dropping the tea bags into the cups to steep. He carried the cups and saucers to the table, moved back to the counter and returned with a sugar bowl and two spoons. Taking a seat across from her, he tried to ignore the way the skin on his arm tingled from her proximity. It really had been a while since he'd been alone with a woman, even in a nonromantic circumstance.

"Okay. Spill."

"It's just that I don't understand why this is so hard. I have all of this expertise with other people's children. I'm good at my job. Really." She tilted her head toward one ear then the other as if weighing the statement. "At least I thought I was. But what kind of social worker can I be if I can't relate to my own child?"

"The classical music probably didn't help."

She frowned as she wrapped the string of her tea bag around her spoon, squeezed out the water then set the bag aside. "Probably not."

"Look, I don't have as much textbook knowledge about teenagers as you do." He took a sip of his tea and then grinned. "Practical knowledge, either. But you would tell me to be patient with Blake, so I'm going to tell you the same thing. He's had a lot of changes to deal with in the past few days."

Her eyes were still too shiny, but her lips pulled up

in something close to a smile. "You're right. I should be telling *you* that."

"So listen to yourself. And don't worry about the time running out. He's here now." He pointed up to indicate upstairs. "That's all that matters."

"And at some point, he might even decide to come down," she said. She lifted her tea to her lips and turned her head away, appearing lost in her thoughts.

"How are you handling this new development in *your* life, anyway?"

She turned back to him. "Have you looked at me tonight? I'm not handling it that well."

Oh, he'd been looking, all right, but he doubted she would want to know how little interest he'd paid to her mental well-being. "I think you're doing all right. It's a lot to digest."

"You act as if it came as a big surprise to me that I had a child." A sad smile spread on her lips. "Believe me, I never forgot it."

"But you never expected him to show up on your doorstep like an overnight delivery, either."

"No. That I didn't expect."

She'd been staring into the cup in front of her as if the deep brown liquid offered answers to her questions, but suddenly Shannon lifted her head and looked right at him. She seemed to be searching for something. Was she trying to decide whether he was just being polite or if he really wanted to know her story? He was surprised to realize that he did want to know. More than he had any right to.

"As I said before, I'd always planned to look for Blake after he turned eighteen. I wasn't even sure how to get started, but I promised myself I would do it. The truth is that it was easy to think of it that way. As something in the future. It felt safe."

Shannon lowered her gaze to her cup again. "I didn't have to admit then that I wasn't ready to face him. To have to explain myself. But then he was right at my door, standing in front of me, and I did and said all of the wrong things."

She squeezed her eyes shut and then opened them again. "I've messed it up now. I don't know what Blake was looking for, but I've disappointed him somehow. I'm worried that I've destroyed any chance for us to build some kind of relationship."

"You don't really believe that, do you?"

Her stark expression as she stirred her tea, though she'd put no sugar in it, suggested that she did believe it.

"Well, you're wrong."

"How do you know?"

"I might not know everything about teens the way you do, but I have to believe that any kid who went to so much trouble to, first, keep a letter from his probable birth mother through several moves and, second, to track her down, wants a relationship with her."

She studied him with a confused expression. "I don't get it."

"Get what?"

"If you truly believe that Blake wants a relationship with me, then why do you keep planting yourself between us? Do you think he needs to be protected from me?"

"No. That's not it." But the words didn't ring true, even to him, because that was exactly what he'd done. He considered giving her some vague answer, but she'd been open with him, so he told her the truth.

"I guess I was just worried about Blake. So many

adults in his life have failed him. I didn't want to be one of them."

"Neither do I," she said automatically, but then she stopped and dragged her front teeth over her bottom lip. "But I already did. I was one of the first."

She closed her eyes and rubbed fingers in a circular motion over her temples. Clearly she'd never needed his blame. She'd been doing a great job of blaming herself.

"You were just a kid yourself then." His words surprised him, but he found he wasn't sorry for saying them. She needed reassurance, and after the way he'd questioned her, she deserved that much.

"If only youth could be a good enough excuse for the stupid things we do." She smiled, but the expression didn't reach her eyes.

"It's as good an excuse as any other. You never said anything about Blake's biological father, other than that he wasn't involved. Was he…uh…as young as you were?"

Mark swallowed. Why was he throwing a question out of left field like that? It was like interviewing a burglary suspect and asking him why he'd murdered his mother. He was supposed to be bolstering Shannon's belief that she could eventually get through to Blake, and he could only ask nosy questions about the boy's deadbeat dad instead.

"Not quite as young. But that's a long story." She straightened in her seat and sipped her tea, though it had to be getting cold by now. "So tell me, why is it that you find it so easy to relate to Blake?"

He looked up at her abrupt change of subject. It was the second time she'd cut off his questions about the guy who'd deserted her. Clearly Blake's birth father was still a sore subject for her, even after all of these years. Mark didn't know why he was so curious about the loser, anyway. Guys who ran off on their pregnant girlfriends were as common as unplanned pregnancies. But this guy had bailed out on this particular woman, and it didn't sit right with him.

"Are you planning to keep it a secret? Why is it so easy?"

He needed to stop daydreaming and give her an answer.

"I already told you I was a delinquent."

"That's it?" She tilted her head to the side. "All delinquents speak some common language? Like punk-speak or something?"

He grinned. "Something like that. With Blake, I just don't pressure him too much."

"And I do?"

Their gazes met, but neither said anything. They both knew the answer to that.

"Were you just a garden-variety delinquent, or did you really get into trouble?"

"Both, I guess. I threw firecrackers in the school trash cans, painted graphic pictures on the high school football field right before Homecoming and shoplifted stuff I didn't want when I had money to pay for it in my pockets."

"Why did you do all of that?"

"I guess it was the only way I could get my parents to notice me and not my annoying, overachieving brothers, Bill and David, and their awards *du jour*."

Shannon drew her eyebrows together. "That's the best story you've got? I work with troubled teens. I can top that story without even breaking the seal on one of the big case files."

"Yeah, I guess it was ordinary delinquent stuff, but

then I really did it." He paused, trying to decide if he should stop altogether. The last person he'd told this story to had walked away from him and all of the promises she'd made to him. Another person he'd managed to disappoint. But somehow it seemed right to tell Shannon. She was like him in that she'd failed some of the people in her life, and her scars were every bit as deep as his.

"When I was fourteen, five of us got drunk and had the brilliant idea of going joyriding through town." He took a deep breath, trying to tell the story without reliving it. "I don't remember anything after I crawled into that car. I woke up in the hospital with only a bump on my head, but our friend, Chris, has been in a wheelchair ever since."

It was as if all of the oxygen had been pulled from the room, and all he could do was hold his breath and wait for her response to his story. He could already sense her judgment in the silence.

"Oh, Mark. That's horrible. I'm so sorry."

He blinked and then released his breath in tiny bursts. He didn't want her to feel sorry for him, so it surprised him how relieved he felt that she hadn't been quick to judge. He tried not to wonder whether she was wasting her compassion on someone who didn't deserve it. Maybe he shouldn't have told her after all. But it had been important to him that she understood the truth about him. He was no hero, even if he'd tried to be one for Blake's sake…and hers.

"I wasn't driving the car," he continued, "but that didn't make a difference, particularly to my parents. They always saw me as the kid from the accident. Chris told me he forgave me, but how could anyone forgive a guy who was able to walk away from his mistakes when he could never walk again?"

"That's why you became a cop, isn't it?" She held her hands wide. "To make up for some of the things you did."

He must not have done a good job at hiding his surprise because she laughed. "Come on, Mark. I had a teenage pregnancy, and I've spent the past five years working at a home for teen moms. I know a little about trying to make up for the past."

"I guess you do."

For a few minutes, they sat in silence, lost in their own memories and regrets, but then Shannon looked up at him.

"Wait. You said 'saw.' Your parents. Are they…?"

"They died in a car accident four years ago. Before— I don't know—before I became what I could be."

She watched him for so long that he had to force himself not to squirm in his seat.

"You've had a lot of loss in your life, even after your friend's injury. Your parents. Your marriage."

He swallowed and sat up straighter. "Those two things aren't the same at all. One was an accident, and the other… Well, you can't *accidentally* cheat on someone."

"Oh. I'm sorry."

"Kim was the one who introduced me to faith in God, and yet she had no problem violating the Ten Commandments. She actually blamed *me* for her cheating, saying I cared more about the police force than her. And then she left me for her trainer at the gym." He waved away the story with a swipe of his hand, wishing it was as easy to brush away the feelings of betrayal and loss. "At least she made a health-conscious choice."

"That's not funny."

"Guess not."

But it wasn't okay either, for him to let her comfort him when he was supposed to be supporting *her*. How had they switched places? She'd probably asked all of those questions to prevent him from asking more about Blake's father, but she hadn't forced him to answer. Hadn't insisted that he gut himself like a salmon and let his secrets drain out on the kitchen table. No, he'd done that all by himself. Now he wanted to drag his innards back in, step away from her and put his guard back up where it belonged. He pushed back from the table and stood.

"Have you checked on Blake lately?" he asked.

"He hasn't come out even once." She jerked her head, looking past him to the hallway leading to the stairs. "Wait. You don't think…?"

"No." He shook his head for emphasis. "He wouldn't have gone out that window. He knows he can't afford to run again. Besides, it's a straight drop to the driveway, and there weren't enough sheets in there for him to tie up to make a prison break."

But just in case, he held his index finger out to indicate that she would wait, and he stealthily climbed the stairs. Flipping on the hall light, he stepped to the closed door and waited, listening for sounds coming from inside the room. Nothing. He tested the knob and found the door unlocked after all. When he pushed open the door, allowing light to flood the room, he found Blake just where he was supposed to be: in the bed pushed against the wall. He was lying on his side, his knees drawn up to his chest, with that old quilt from Mark's parents' home pulled up to just under his nose.

More relieved than he cared to admit, he backed quietly out of the room and right into Shannon.

"Ooomf," she said, when his elbow made contact with her stomach.

"I told you to wait," he whispered. "What are you doing—"

But she wasn't listening. She was staring at her son, her eyes glistening in the soft light.

"The last time I saw him sleeping…"

Her whispered words trailed away then, but Mark had no doubt she could picture that last time when he would have been just a newborn, either in her arms or behind glass in the hospital nursery. He wanted to know which, wanted to be able to picture the story clearly himself, but her expression was so stark that he couldn't bring himself to ask. Whichever image burned vividly in her memory right now, nearly fifteen years afterward, the boy slept on, oblivious to the light pouring in from the hall and the muffled voices outside the door.

"He preferred to be in here, alone, all night, than to spend time…with me."

Her voice caught on the last, and her anguish was so palpable that he could feel the ache of it inside his heart.

"Everything's going to work out with him. You've got to believe that."

But she only shook her head, her eyes filling again. "I don't deserve a second chance, do I?"

"Wait." Somehow he managed to keep his voice low as he pulled the door closed. "Of course you deserve a second chance. We all do."

He didn't remember reaching for her hand as she braced it on the edge of the door frame, but it was suddenly there, his wide hand covering her tiny one so completely that it was shielded from view. As he squeezed her hand, it exuded warmth that seeped right into his skin. A tingle raced from his fingertips to his shoulder.

As if that wasn't enough to tell him he'd made a mistake by touching her, when he looked away from their hands, his gaze only locked with hers. She stared at him with wide eyes. It was just a second, maybe a fraction of a second, and yet there was an awareness between them that hadn't been there minutes before. Her light floral scent, her halted breathing, the slight rush of her pulse inundated his senses. Confused him.

Terrified him.

What was he doing? The ink wasn't even dry on his divorce papers, and here he was not only thinking about a woman, but *touching* one. And not just any woman either, but one with a history of walking away from her own child. He'd just told her that she deserved a second chance, and as a Christian, he should be forgiving, but her track record still made him nervous.

Clearing his throat, he pulled his hand away and stepped back. Shannon looked away for several seconds and then lowered her hand from the wall.

"Um, I'd better be getting home."

"Okay. We'll be over early tomorrow to work on those gutters."

"Sounds good."

Already she'd started down the stairs. Away from him. By the time Mark reached the landing, he'd done a pretty effective job at convincing himself that whatever had just passed between them was all in his head. And if it wasn't, well, he'd better forget about it, anyway.

He had to return to Hope Haven tomorrow, but he promised himself he would keep his distance from Shannon Lyndon by only doing outside jobs. No one had ever put Blake first. Mark was determined to be the one to do it. He would focus on teaching Blake new skills as they completed home repairs. He would help him prepare for classes at his new school next week, and he would encourage him to consider building a relationship with Shannon. Yes, he would put the boy first in everything he did this week, if he could only keep his thoughts away from Blake's mother.

Chapter Seven

Holding her breath, Shannon slowly turned the key in the back door lock, but the click pierced the rural silence like a gunshot. She jumped, managing not to fall off the back porch. The door creaked as she opened it, allowing in a sliver of light from the porch lamp. Even knowing the exact location of the squeaky floorboard didn't help her to avoid stepping on it. Good thing Katie had remembered not to set the alarm tonight after she'd sent the girls to bed, or that would have been blaring, too.

Why was she sneaking, anyway? She was an adult. She didn't have a curfew. She had nothing to feel guilty about, either. Her girls were under Katie's capable care and probably had been asleep for hours. Why was it so important to her that no one knew what time she returned home? Memories of other clandestine moments stole into her mind, but she closed her eyes, forcing them from view. Her thoughts had been confusing enough without her dredging more sludge from the past.

What had just happened between her and Mark? She wasn't sure, but one thing she did know was that there'd been so many sparks in that upstairs hallway that her hair should have caught on fire. His hand over hers had felt so warm, so strong, that she couldn't help but imagine what it would feel like if he drew her into his arms. Had he felt the electricity, too? She didn't bother telling herself that she'd imagined it when she'd practically raced from the house to escape the energy of it. Even after fifteen minutes in time and traveling distance to her home, she remained a mass of disturbed nerve endings.

Shivering, though she was still wearing her coat, she closed the door, flipped the lock and reached for the kitchen light switch. Fluorescent light flooded the room before she could touch the switch plate. Squealing, she jumped again, this time knocking her elbow against the countertop.

"Sorry, Miss Shannon." Brooke stood in the doorway, a robe tied over pajamas, fuzzy slippers on her feet. "You had a late night."

Shannon shrugged out of her coat and hung it on one of the hooks by the door. "I told you all that I would be staying with Blake sometimes until Mark—I mean, Trooper Shoffner—comes home from work."

"He works late."

The teen was probably just making an observation, yet it felt like an accusation. Shannon shouldn't have stayed so late with Mark, even if he'd been sweet to offer her tea and a listening ear. "It won't always be that late."

It wouldn't have been so late this time if she hadn't kept asking him more about his past. At first, she'd only posed the questions to avoid answering his, but then he'd started talking and she couldn't get enough of his stories. She'd completely taken his side, too. Even before his trip to check on Blake, she'd already been wondering what kind of parents never forgave their son, and, worse yet, how any woman could have left a great guy like Mark.

"How much did Blake love having a babysitter?"

Shannon swallowed, caught ruminating over matters she'd had no business thinking about then...or remembering now. "About as much as you'd expect." Maybe she was the one who'd needed a babysitter tonight.

As Brooke stood leaning against the door frame, Shannon half expected the rest of the girls to crowd around her and pepper her with questions. The hallway behind Brooke, though, remained in shadow.

"What are you doing up so late, anyway? The baby needs you to get your rest."

Brooke rubbed a hand near her collarbone and then allowed her arm to rest on the upper curve of her abdomen. "Heartburn. I haven't been sleeping that well lately. My feet are swelling, too."

"Yeah, all of the fun side effects of pregnancy." Shannon smiled, remembering. "Near the end, it was so hard to get comfortable enough to sleep."

Brooke smiled back at her. "I'm glad that you're finally able to share your own experiences with us, but I understand that you had a right to keep your secret."

"Thanks. I'm glad, too." She realized she was only responding to one of Brooke's comments, but she'd cried enough for one day. Still, an enormous lump clogged her throat, refusing to budge.

When she followed the teen through the door into the dining area, she noticed the plate, glass of milk and box of graham crackers Brooke had already placed on one of the tables there.

Shannon indicated the snacks with a wave of her hand. "I doubt those are going to help your heartburn."

"Yeah, but Parasite here was hungry again." She

pointed to her stomach and then slowly lowered herself into a chair.

Shannon nodded. In a group like this, it was common for the girls to nickname their babies, but she'd never been a fan of that particular moniker. "Well, clean up after yourself, and try to get back to bed. You'll be exhausted for your class work tomorrow. Weren't you studying for a chemistry midterm?"

The girl only rolled her eyes. "Yes, Mom."

"Well, good night. I have to set the alarm." Shannon started toward the hall.

"Miss Shannon," Brooke called after her.

She glanced back to find the teen sitting with her arms crossed over her stomach, her expression giving nothing away. The snack and milk in front of her remained untouched.

"Were you sorry you did it?"

Shannon turned to face her. There was more to the girl's late-night-snack mission after all. "You mean the adoption?"

She nodded.

Because this conversation was going to take a while and because she needed time to decide how to answer, Shannon joined her at the table. Still not eating, the girl sat staring at her hands.

"We've talked about how each situation is different," Shannon began. "Each young mother must decide what is right for her, her baby and her family."

She paused, waiting for the girl to say something, but when she didn't look up, Shannon tried again. "And I've told you what a wonderful, unselfish choice you've made in placing your baby with a loving family. Your baby will be a gift from God for a couple who've been praying for a child to love."

This time Brooke met her gaze and shook her head. "I'm not talking about *our* choices. I'm asking about *yours*."

Shannon swallowed, though it shouldn't have surprised her that one of the girls had asked. What should have surprised her more was that it had taken one of them this long to do it.

"I didn't want to place my baby for adoption, but I didn't feel as if I had a choice," she said finally. "My parents insisted on adoption, and I let them convince me that it was the right thing to do… I mean, the right thing for me."

She cringed, wishing she'd kept her mouth shut. The last thing she wanted to do was to make Brooke or any of the girls question their decisions based on hers. But she'd dug this hole, so she started backfilling. "I want you to know that the whole thing about Blake's adoptive parents losing parental rights, that was… Well, an anomaly. About as likely as prospective adoptive parents deciding they didn't want a baby after all."

To her surprise, Brooke chuckled.

"Don't worry, Miss Shannon. I still believe that people should live in houses, even though sometimes houses are hit by tornadoes. They should drive cars, even though sometimes they hit brick walls." She finally took a bite of her graham cracker and washed it down with a swallow of milk. "Parasite's folks will be great."

"I'm sure they will be." Shannon pushed up from the table. "Anyway, I need to get to bed. And I know you need to."

This time Brooke stood with her and collected her dishes and the box of crackers.

"Well, good night." She drew the girl in for a hug.

"Thanks for telling me some of your story. I'd won-

dered why it was so important to you that we each had
the chance to decide for ourselves whether we wanted
to keep our babies or place them for adoption." Brooke
smiled. "Now I know."

The conversation followed her as Shannon moved to
the entry and set the house alarm. She'd admitted that
the choice regarding Blake's adoption hadn't really been
hers, but she had a choice now, and she was choosing to
be a mother to him, if he would only let her. Blake was
the sole reason that she and Mark were collaborating.
She couldn't lose sight of that by allowing herself to
develop romantic notions about Blake's foster dad, no
matter how generous and kind he seemed to be. Mark
was only there for Blake's sake, and she needed to remember that. Otherwise, she risked failing to connect
with her son the way she needed to, and when he was
placed elsewhere, she would again be that thing she
dreaded most. Alone.

"Are you sure you'll be able to finish this by Wednesday? We'll need this room for Thursday."

Shannon indicated the paneled walls of the basement
recreation room, the area that she'd been planning to
paint for two years. Since none of the girls could help
because they shouldn't be exposed to the paint fumes,
she'd never found the time to do it.

Mark didn't even look back from the wall, where he
was using filling compound to repair nail holes. "Well,
it's inside instead of out there in the rain, so at least we
have a chance of finishing *something* this week."

As tightly as she was wound today, she wouldn't accomplish much herself no matter where she was. She'd
told herself to steer clear of Mark, but her warnings had
no effect now that he was here in the flesh rather than

in theory. Even her suspicion that she'd imagined that whole moment between them last night didn't help. If one of the girls sneaked up behind her and tapped her shoulder, she would probably go *pop,* her limbs shooting every which way in an unfortunate gymnastics feat.

"I know you wanted to work on the gutters, but…"

"Doesn't matter," Mark said with a sigh. "But if it doesn't stop raining soon, your guests will have to paddle to Thanksgiving dinner in canoes."

"You're positive you can have it finished?"

Blake turned back to her, still holding the scraper he was using to remove loose paint. "We probably could do that without so many interruptions."

Clearly Mark wasn't the only one annoyed that they couldn't work outside today. Or maybe just that they couldn't get away from her.

"Blake," Mark said in a warning tone, "that is not an acceptable way for you to speak to an adult."

The boy turned his head slightly to the side. "Sorry."

Without saying more, Blake returned to his work. How would she ever reach him if he refused to give her the chance? But the two paint cans, drop cloths, rollers and brushes stacked in the corner gave her an idea.

"I'll be back in a few minutes."

She had to laugh at their unenthusiastic grunts of acknowledgment as she ascended the stairs. When she returned just minutes later in work clothes and grabbed a paintbrush, neither guy said anything at all.

"I thought it might go faster if the three of us worked together." If nothing else, this was a way of supporting Mark's work with Blake as he'd supported hers last night. That she wouldn't have to make excuses to be in the same room as them was a bonus.

"It's your house," Mark said finally.

It wasn't an engraved invitation, but it would have to do. He seemed as reluctant to spend time with her as she was supposed to be with him today. But, of course, she was only there to see Blake when he couldn't hide in his bedroom, so what Mark wanted shouldn't matter. She set up camp not far from where Blake was using a damp sponge to wipe down the walls he'd been scraping.

"My parents always made me help them paint rooms when I was a kid." She slid a glance Blake's way to see if he was listening. "Did you ever do any painting at your...homes?"

"Yeah, a few of them required slave labor."

Inwardly, she groaned. Why hadn't she thought before asking that question?

But Mark only chuckled. "Slave labor, Blake? If you're so experienced at it, you'll know exactly how today's going to go. But here we call it *community service.*"

"Same difference."

"At least the girls picked an interesting color." Shannon used the paint key to open the can of cerulean paint. "My mom always picked colors with names like linen or peaches and cream."

Another grunt from Blake would have been better than his stony silence. From across the room, Mark whistled a familiar tune. When she recognized it as the old hymn, "The Garden," she smiled. If she'd ever needed a reminder that she wasn't alone—that God was with her—it was these past few days. He'd placed Mark in their lives for a reason, as well. And maybe through Mark she would finally be able to share her story with her son.

She poured a small amount of paint into a tray and closed the can, but instead of settling in her original spot, she carried the tray and a brush to the corner closer to Mark. "Okay to start here?"

"As good as anywhere," he said.

She dipped the brush and smoothed long strokes of the sky-blue paint in the corner. "I would have loved to paint my childhood bedroom a color like this, but my parents never would have allowed it."

"Why not?" Mark asked as if he understood his role in the conversation without her laying it out for him.

"It wouldn't have measured up to their standards of perfection. Just like I didn't."

She was desperate to know if Blake was listening, but she couldn't look at him, not and say what needed to be said. "I jumped through hoops at home, school and church to meet their impossible expectations. But none of the things I did were ever good enough. So you can imagine how they reacted when they found out that their only daughter was pregnant."

"What did they do?"

She understood that Mark was playing along so she could tell her story, so it startled her that his interest appeared genuine.

"They were ashamed of me and didn't want anyone in our church to know about my pregnancy, so they shipped me away to my grandmother's until the birth. I wanted…I wanted to keep my baby, but they were relentless." She focused on the paint as she smoothed it on the wall, but her throat felt thick and heavy. Her eyes burned.

"They said I should think of the baby first. That adoption was the right thing to do. That it was selfish of me to want to keep my child. When those arguments didn't convince me, they told me not to expect any support from them if I brought a baby home."

"So you felt that you didn't have a choice."

Mark didn't look at her as he said it, but his words bolstered her. Was Blake really hearing her, too? Did he understand just a little?

"When it looked as though I would give in, they assured me that I would be able to go on with my life." She dipped the brush into the paint again, swirling it round and round. "They said no one would have to know. But they didn't warn me that no matter what, I would always know what I'd done."

Mark didn't say anything right away, making her wonder if she'd said too much. Finally, though, he lowered his putty knife, resting it on top of the tub of goop. "Thanks for telling me your story, but I was still wondering something. If you kept your pregnancy a secret from almost everyone, did you ever tell Blake's father?"

She gave him a sharp look. Why did Mark have to keep asking about Scott? Why was it so important to him to know about Blake's father? But then she peeked at Blake, who'd paused from wiping the wall as if he didn't want to miss what was being said. Suddenly, it made sense to her. Of course, Blake would want to know about his father. Mark had allowed her to use him as part of her information relay system, and now he was asking questions Blake would want answered. Though she wasn't ready to share everything—she might never be—she would tell Blake as much as she could.

"Yes, I told him, but he wasn't…ready to be a dad." She closed her eyes, took a deep breath and started again. "His name is Scott Turner. He was just a kid, too. I guess I would call him the bad boy. Everyone else did. Anyway, he pretty much disappeared after I told him I was pregnant."

"What do you mean *pretty much?*" Mark asked.

"He made sure that my parents knew where to find him so he could sign off on the voluntary release of parental rights."

"Oh. Where is he now?"

Having painted as high as she could reach without a stepladder, she sat on the aged linoleum floor and brushed strokes in a line just above the base molding. "It would make a more interesting story to say he's in prison or something, but I don't really know where he is."

Blake rinsed his sponge in a bucket of water and started wiping again, but since he continued to clean the same spot, he wasn't making much progress.

"So you haven't kept tabs on him?"

Mark asked the question too casually, and Shannon's pulse took a humiliating stutter step. She couldn't allow herself to start thinking that the officer might be jealous of a guy in her past. Mark was only here for Blake, just as everything he'd done had been for Blake alone. Even his kindness to her last night was ultimately for Blake's benefit so that the boy could develop a relationship with his mother.

"About five years ago I heard that he was doing construction work in Colorado. But let's just say he and I don't exchange Christmas cards."

Mark nodded, appearing satisfied with her answers. She could only hope Blake was, as well.

"You're right. Prison would have made for a more entertaining story." He turned and pointed to her with a sheet of sandpaper in his hand. "Hey, I can check his criminal record on LEIN—uh, the Law Enforcement Information Network—if you like."

"Thanks, but that won't be necessary."

"The offer stands." He brushed his hand over a spot

on the wall to make sure that the compound had dried and sanded it smooth. "A lot of bad boys pull it together when they grow up, anyway. I know I did."

"Maybe you just weren't as bad as you thought you were."

"That could be right." He gave her a mean look. "All I'm saying is that it's possible for people to turn their lives around if they really want to. Maybe that has happened for this...Scott."

Shannon's hand jerked where she'd been painting, causing several droplets to land on the floor. She dabbed at the spots with a piece of wet paper towel. Again, she questioned Mark's comments. What was he trying to do, convince Blake to track down his birth father the same way he'd located her? Especially now that she'd given him the name. But she reasoned, as Mark probably had, that encouraging Blake to idolize his birth father like some Al Capone–type character wasn't the best idea, either. What if he decided to follow in the family tradition?

"I'm sure he turned his life around," she said with all of the confidence she could muster.

When she caught Mark's eye again, he nodded. Strange how his approval of her interactions with her son had become so important to her. She was supposed to be guiding him, and from the start, Mark had been instructing her. If she didn't find something to teach him soon, she would feel downright obsolete.

"If we're painting this room to get it ready for the big Thanksgiving shindig, what preparations are the girls doing upstairs?"

Mark's words drew her back into the conversation. He seemed to understand that as much as she'd longed to share her story with her son, they'd spent enough time tromping around in the past for one day. Enough time leaving footprints over long-shielded memories. Relaxing for the first time since Mark and Blake had arrived this morning, Shannon took hold of the new, safer topic with both hands.

"Oh, the girls are just as busy as we are," she told him. "They each have a list of special chores to complete after their class work is finished. They'll also help me with the baking and cooking."

"It sounds like a big deal."

As if Blake recognized that none of the new information applied to him, he set his sponge aside, grabbed a roller and crouched to pour paint into a pan.

"At the rate you guys are going, we'll still be painting this room at Christmas," he grumbled as he wet the roller and started painting the spot Shannon had already framed in.

"Wouldn't want that," Mark said with a chuckle. He winked at Shannon. "Is the Thanksgiving thing something you plan every year?"

She tried to ignore the butterflies fluttering in her stomach over something as minor as a wink. What was she, an eighth grader? "This is the third time. It's something for each new group of girls to look forward to while they're living here. We invite their families, and we usually have a nice turnout."

She moved farther down the wall and kept painting along that molding. "The girls don't get out much, other than taking turns joining one of the adults on grocery shopping trips or going with us on group outings to the movies or museums."

"Do they ever have visitors?"

"Not many. Some of the parents are able to stop by on weekends and take their daughters out for dinner, but since our residents come from all over the state—a few outside the state—most parents can't visit often."

She didn't mention that some of the parents who never visited lived no more than thirty minutes away in bad traffic. Those were the same ones who'd already sent their regrets for Thursday. They and her own parents, who coincidentally or intentionally had been away on mission trips each time she'd hosted one of the events.

"What about their…guys?"

She grinned at his discomfort in asking about the young fathers. "They're allowed to visit on weekends as long as they come with the residents' parents. They also can call or text during nonclassroom time, but they seldom do that, either. For most of the girls who agree to come here, their boyfriends are already a distant memory, or will be right after their babies are born."

"Wait." Mark cocked his head to the side. "Didn't Trooper Davison say he was called here for a domestic involving one of the dads?"

"That was about a year ago. The young man showed up to have a shouting match in the front yard with a fifteen-year-old resident. He accused her of lying when she named him as her baby's 'putative,' or commonly accepted, father in the legal documents. A beautiful moment."

"Hmm. Sounds like it."

She didn't know about that moment, but this one had become more pleasant than it had any right to be. With Mark's help, she'd finally been able to make Blake listen to her side of the story, but it was more than that. She liked talking to Mark, enjoyed hearing what he had to say. She never forgot that Blake was right there, pretending not to listen to their conversation, but she found that she wouldn't mind if it were just Mark and her. Alone.

That wasn't a good idea, and she knew it. She shouldn't allow herself to become attracted to Mark Shoffner, not when she finally had the chance to form a relationship with Blake. But in truth she already *was* attracted, and in a way she hadn't been drawn to anyone in years. Not since Scott. And only as an adult could she look back on that young relationship and understand that attraction was all she'd had then.

But this thing with Mark was more than attraction. She genuinely liked him as a person, wanted to know what he thought and was convinced that he would make a great friend. This was dangerous. Because liking him tempted her to open herself up to him, to let him know the real her. To make herself vulnerable. She'd taken that kind of risk only once before, leaving her heart exposed, and she still bore the scars from it, both inside and on the outside from the emergency cesarean section. And vulnerable was the thing she'd promised herself she would never be again.

Chapter Eight

"Here. I can get that for you."

Blake bent over Kelly's much shorter frame and lifted a tray of cut-up sandwiches from her arms. He indicated the cafeteria area with a tilt of his head. "Where do you want me to put it?"

She pointed to a long table. Trays of fruit and vegetables and cups of yogurt were spaced along it beside pitchers of milk and plastic cups.

"I could have done that myself, you know."

"I know. I just wanted to help a little."

"Okay." But she narrowed her gaze at him.

Shannon had to grin at Kelly's suspicious reaction to Blake's chivalry. After what the girls had been through, she couldn't blame them for questioning the motives of teenage boys. As for Blake's comment about helping, he'd already done more than "a little" of that while they'd prepared for lunch. He'd unstacked most of the chairs and moved tables from against the wall in the cafeteria area that doubled as an activity room for their prenatal exercise classes.

If Kelly's suspicion bothered him, he didn't let on that it did. He only started back through the swinging doors into the kitchen and wrestled a tray from another girl's hands. Shannon was tempted to remind him that the girls were pregnant—not invalids. But she was too proud of how sweet he was being to the girls, who often faced unkind comments from others, to say anything. It hadn't been a bad idea to invite Mark and Blake to join them for lunch after all.

"You see," Mark whispered. "You shouldn't have worried about having Blake around the girls."

Shannon shivered as his warm breath tickled her neck. How he could have been able to sneak up behind her, she couldn't imagine, since she was usually overly sensitive to his presence. "I wasn't worried. Not much, anyway."

"He's great with them." Mark's gaze followed Blake as he emerged from the kitchen again, carrying a tray of cookies.

Several of the girls had already lined up at one end of the table the way they normally did, and Blake took a spot at the end of the line.

"But he's been a curmudgeon all day," Shannon said.

Someone must have said something entertaining then because Blake actually smiled.

"Curmudgeon, huh?" Mark said. "And you were worried that he would bring all of that sweetness to the girls. No, Mom, he reserves that delightful behavior just for you."

He'd been joking, but it was the first time Mark had ever referred to her as Blake's mother in any way, though he clearly believed she was. Even the DNA maternity test they'd scheduled for that afternoon was only a formality for later court proceedings. Her throat tightened. Hearing Mark say it was almost as great as she imagined it would be if—when—Blake would say it. Like a vote of confidence in a room filled with nos.

She cleared her throat. "So I'm the privileged one?"

"Yes, that's you."

As the line became shorter, Mark and Shannon stepped to the end of it and started filling their plates. They paused as Chelsea took her turn saying grace so those who were already seated could start eating while the others finished getting their food in line.

"The girls appear to be on their best behavior, too," Mark said as he lifted his tray after the amen.

She raised an eyebrow and waited for him to explain.

"You were worried about that, too, weren't you?"

Guilt filled her as she glanced at the girls seated in groups of three or four. How could she have been concerned that her girls might be inappropriately flirtatious with Blake around? She was supposed to be one of the few people who was always on their side, who always believed in their potential and didn't define them by their mistakes.

"I just didn't know how they would react to having a guy here. Even Miss Lafferty told us this was no place for a teenage boy."

"It was more him *living* here that she had a problem with," he said with a chuckle.

Ahead of them, Blake poured a glass of milk, but as he started toward the tables, he paused, uncertain.

"Come eat with us, Blake," Brooke called out. She indicated an empty seat between hers and Chelsea's. "Don't sit with the boring adults."

Blake glanced back at Mark, and, at his nod, he joined the girls at the table. As he sat down, Brooke introduced him to a few of the girls he had yet to meet, and then just when he lifted his hand to wave at them, she reached over and messed up his hair as one would a younger brother. His face turned crimson, and he shoved his hair out of his eyes.

Shannon released the breath she'd been holding. Her son might have a tough-guy persona, but he was no ladies' man yet. As she led Mark to one of the other tables, the familiar din of competing conversations filled the room. Although she busied herself removing the plate, cup and silverware from her tray, she still couldn't resist peeking over at the table where Blake sat with the girls. Strange how she'd memorized every one of the residents' birthdays, but they'd never seemed as young as they did sitting next to Blake. Particularly Chelsea, who must have said something funny because they all started laughing.

"I think they'll be safe during lunch. But we'll be here in case mayhem ensues."

Caught again, Shannon gave him a mean look and then grinned. He smiled back, their gazes connecting only for a second, but her cheeks still warmed. Wetting her suddenly dry lips, she looked away. And she saw them. All of the people who mattered most to her were right here together. The child whose heart had first fluttered inside of her own body. The girls who had each stolen a piece of her heart.

The scary thing was that she was tempted to include Mark in that group, too. But she couldn't go there. This afternoon would be one of the most critical so far for her and Blake. They would be tested at the hospital to prove that they were truly biologically connected, and then she would meet with the attorney to determine steps toward her ultimate goal of making a home for herself and her son.

Besides, if she was looking for a relationship with a

man right now—and she wasn't—she wouldn't choose someone who still hadn't gotten over his last relationship. Mark might have been divorced, but he was still holding on to his anger over his wife's betrayal. He believed he'd played no role in the demise of his marriage when even as an outsider, she couldn't help but wonder whether or not that was true.

She couldn't lose sight of what was most important here anyway, and the only thing that could matter was that she would be with her son. Just her and Blake. It was the only thing she'd ever wanted, and whether it felt like it at this second or not, it had to be enough.

On Wednesday afternoon, Mark hammered the lid onto the can of glossy white cabinet paint, whacking the hammer several more times though the lid was already good and tight. What was wrong with him? He'd promised himself he would keep his distance from Shannon for Blake's sake, and there probably wasn't a scale to measure how badly he'd failed in the past two days.

Any opportunity to work on her side of the room, any chance to volunteer to help her move furniture or rinse paint rollers, he'd stepped right up. He was out of comedic material now because he'd told every knock-knock joke he could remember just to see her smile or hear her laugh. Even knowing that she'd only been having those conversations with him so that Blake could overhear them hadn't prevented him from enjoying every minute of them. Now they were finished painting the walls and putting an extra coat of paint on the white floor moldings, and he was tempted to find another excuse to spend time with her.

He knew better than to become involved with a woman like Shannon. She'd held on to her blame against her parents for fifteen years. She saw herself as a victim rather than taking responsibility for her own actions. No different from Kim, the suspects he took into custody and even all of the other guys in that car accident so long ago, she blamed everyone but herself. Instead of sending him running in the other direction, though, her weaknesses drew him in, just like everything else about her did.

Maybe it was a good thing that they would be taking off early today so that Shannon could start baking with the girls for tomorrow's event. The only way he would ever get some perspective in this situation would be to put some time and some space between them. He wasn't usually a fan of holidays, most of which he had to work, but this break that Thanksgiving would provide couldn't have come at a more necessary time.

"It looks great, don't you think?" Shannon leaned against the back of the sofa that was still covered with a sheet as she admired their work.

"If you like big blue magic markers...sure."

She only smiled. "The girls are going to love it."

"I think it's all right," Blake chimed, almost as a reminder that he was still there.

Mark shrugged. "Must be a kid thing."

As if to test his premise, three of the girls made their way down the stairs then. Chelsea appeared at the bottom first.

"Are you finished, Miss Shannon? Mrs. Wright let us out of class work early. I got to log off right in the middle of my genetics study guide for bio." But then Chelsea stopped and looked around. "This looks amazing. Oh, hi, Blake. Did you help paint?" She indicated the big blue room with a sweep of her hand.

He nodded but then looked at the ground, the color on his cheeks a deep red.

Kelly followed Chelsea down the stairs, stopping at the bottom step. "I love this." But then she crossed her arms, shivering. "It's freezing in here."

Shannon indicated the open egress window. "The fumes. We had to air the place out."

"But you'll be done soon, right?" Kelly asked. "We need to get started."

"As soon as we get everything cleaned up in here." Already Shannon was pulling the old sheet off the sofa.

"You go on ahead with the girls." Mark held out his arms and caught the sheet when she threw it to him. "We can finish this."

Scanning the paint pans, brushes and roller frames that still needed to be washed and put away, Shannon chewed her lip. "If you're sure…"

"Yeah. Go."

Kelly literally bounced with excitement. "Miss Shannon's going to teach us how to make pumpkin pies. Mine's going to be beautiful."

"My mom makes pumpkin pie and apple pie." Chelsea wore a wistful expression, as if reliving family celebrations during easier times. "She can't make it tomorrow."

"Sorry to hear that," Mark said automatically.

She stared out the basement window, blinking a few times, and then turned back to Mark. "What are you two doing for Thanksgiving? Miss Shannon, we should invite them to our Thanksgiving celebration."

"Yeah. Can we invite them?" Kelly chimed in.

Shannon stared at them as if they'd just announced a plan to implode the Hope Haven house. It might have been entertaining watching her try to maneuver herself out of the situation if Mark hadn't realized right then that as Blake's guardian he should have made some sort of official holiday plans for the two of them. Great foster dad he was turning out to be. He'd expected to have no bigger worries tomorrow than where to find the best carryout turkey and dressing. He'd never considered that the boy might have been hoping for a real holiday dinner.

Once a disappointment, always a disappointment. Mark just changed the individuals he was letting down.

"We'll already have about forty people here for Thanksgiving dinner," Shannon said finally.

Since Mark would have expected her to jump at the chance to spend her first Thanksgiving with Blake, her noncommittal comment surprised him. Just when he was convinced that she really wanted to be a mother to Blake, now she appeared to be backing away. Maybe he was right to worry in the first place.

"So what's two more?" Chelsea asked.

"It's not that…" Shannon's gaze darted to Mark's as she stalled. "It's just that it's last-minute, and Trooper Shoffner and Blake probably already have plans."

So that was it. She'd experienced enough rejection from Blake this week, and she didn't want to get her hopes up when the boy was sure to say no.

Kelly stepped closer and then had to lean her head back to look up to Mark. "Well, Trooper Shoffner, do you?"

"Have plans?" he asked, stalling like Shannon had.

Should he tell her that they would be joining Bill and David and their families in Iron River? He could make that happen with a phone call and about nine hours of driving time, but he hadn't planned to introduce Blake to his übersuccessful brothers and their accomplished wives and kids until he'd at least transformed the delinquent into a model citizen. Or maybe a Rhodes Scholar.

"You know, turkey, cranberry sauce…." Chelsea lifted an eyebrow and waited.

He put the last paint roller in a trash bag. "I just thought we'd make it a casual day. We can watch some football, and Wildwood Diner will be open, so…"

"So nothing."

It was the first time Blake had spoken since the girls had entered the room, so Mark gave him his full attention.

"Come on. It's a real dinner." Blake kept his voice low. He tilted his head to the side a few times, mimicking the motion of pulling Mark along with him.

He had to give the boy that. There was something to be said for a good home-cooked meal, which they wouldn't get at his place. Still, that didn't mean they needed to invade the celebration at Hope Haven. The event promised to be as emotionally charged as any of the moments between Shannon and Blake, even without the magnetic pull between the housemother and himself thrown into the mix.

"Good. Then it's settled." Kelly danced around the room.

"We wouldn't want to intrude." Mark didn't mention that Shannon hadn't officially invited them.

Shannon shook her head. "Forgive my manners. We'd love it if you two could join us." She paused, her gaze on Blake, before turning back to the girls.

"But this event is for you girls," she said. "Are you sure you want to extend the celebration to more people than just you and your families?"

Chelsea nodded, though she grimaced then and

rubbed a place on her tummy where her baby must have kicked. "You invited *your* parents, didn't you?"

"I already told you about their mission trip to Guatemala, didn't I?" Shannon waited for their nods and then continued. "So it will just be the twelve of you and your families. The ones who can come, anyway. Plus the other staff and their families."

"Blake is *your* family."

At Chelsea's softly spoken words, Shannon's hand went to her mouth. Her eyes shone, and the emotion in them was so raw that her anguish gripped Mark inside his gut. She wanted them there, all right, so much so that she was tempted to beg. Of course she would want to spend the holiday with her son. So why couldn't he help wishing that she had the same kind of longing to see *him* there?

"That's right," Kelly said, having missed Shannon's reaction. "And Trooper Shoffner is... Well, Blake's family. At least for now."

Mark swallowed. He was in this, all right. Deeper than he had any right to be. Shannon's gaze met his then, and if she'd asked him to become the new executive director of the Hope Haven, he would have agreed to that, too.

"Then thank you for the invitation. We accept. Let us know when dinner is, and we'll be here two hours early."

Chapter Nine

When the doorbell rang the next morning, Shannon looked up from the sofa pillows she'd just fluffed for the third time and groaned. Automatically, her hands went to her hair, still wrapped in a towel. Not two hours early, but *three*. If only she could have skittered off to her room the way the girls, who'd been working in their pajamas, did.

So much for her plan to have everything ready, her included, before they—before any of the guests—came. Okay, maybe it wasn't such a bad thing that her parents wouldn't be around for this particular holiday. She'd just found Blake, and she wasn't ready to share him yet. Would they reject her son again? She didn't even want to think about that, but she couldn't help wondering if they would reject Mark, too, because of his divorce.

She shook her head and then tightened her towel. Of course her parents had no reason to *accept* Mark. As Kelly had said yesterday, he was Blake's family. Not hers. And the sooner she finally accepted that, the better.

Smoothing her hands over the apron that covered her

black special-occasion dress, she crossed to the front door and pulled it open.

"Happy Thanksgiving," Mark and Blake chorused.

They stood on the porch, their arms laden with food though she'd told them they didn't need to bring anything.

"You going to let us in or what?" Mark shifted a casserole dish in his arms. "This stuff is getting heavy."

"It's cold out here, too." Blake gave an exaggerated shiver.

"Oh. Right." She backed away from the door to allow them inside.

Blake indicated her towel with a tilt of his head. "New style?"

"A *too-early* style."

"Yeah. Sorry."

Instead of waiting for her to direct him, Blake started down the hall toward the kitchen.

Mark followed him but turned back, grimacing. "Sorry. Really. Blake has been bouncing off the walls for two hours, asking when we could leave. I know it's bad for parents to give in to begging, but he wore me down."

Even humiliated to be wearing a towel as an accessory to her dress, she couldn't help smiling at that. Until now he hadn't shown any parenting weakness since he'd opened his home to Blake nearly a week before.

"We'll have to work on that, but—" She glanced down the hall to where Blake had disappeared. "He was excited about coming *here* today?"

"Oh, he would never admit that, but he was up at the crack of dawn, forcing me to take him to the grocery store that should have been closed on the holiday but wasn't." He shrugged, allowing the bags to shift on his arms. "Did I mention they were heavy?"

Frowning, she led Mark into the kitchen and helped him find places for the food on the counter, along with all of the serving dishes and platters. The succulent scent of roasting turkeys already wafted from the industrial ovens. "Did you make that yourself?" She indicated the casserole dish containing baked macaroni and cheese with a topping of dried breadcrumbs.

"Of course I did. I do know how to read a recipe." He glanced back from the counter. "I ended up with several of my mother's recipes after she died."

His gaze lowered to the dish he set on a hot pad, and then he looked back at her again. She swallowed, touched that he'd made one of his mother's recipes for their celebration.

"It was nice of you to go to so much trouble. I did tell you not to, though." She scanned the various cans and boxes he'd brought along. Some they could use today and others she'd be challenged to ever find a use for, but the thought definitely counted.

"No trouble."

"Whatever you say." She accepted his story, though with all he'd done, he couldn't have had much more sleep than she'd had.

"Okay. What now?" he asked.

"What do you mean?"

"We're here to help you get ready for the celebration, so just let us know what still needs to be done."

She pushed through the swinging door to the cafeteria area and indicated for him to follow. Blake was already out there, so full of nervous energy that he was pacing.

"We're going to line up all of the tables into two long

ones and then cover them with those white tablecloths."
She pointed to a stack on the counter. "The girls will
be down to help you in a few minutes. They decided to
get dressed early."

"I wonder why." Mark grinned, watching Blake's
return trip down the length of the room. "Wait. Where
are you going? You didn't invite us as a ploy so you
could slip out and have a holiday of solitude, did you?"

"And miss all of this? The girls love this day, and so
do I." She would love it even more this time, but she was
determined not to cry today so she didn't mention that.

"You didn't answer the question."

"In case you hadn't noticed, I still have to get ready."
She pulled the towel off her head and let her hair fall
down in a messy heap.

He studied her for several seconds, as if he was only
now noticing that she hadn't been ready to receive
guests. "You look fine just the way you are."

"And you're saying that to be nice because you're
getting a free Thanksgiving dinner out of this." Her
words sounded rushed, nervous to her, so she didn't try
to convince herself that he didn't notice it.

But he only smiled and repeated her words from earlier. "Whatever you say."

Excusing herself from the room, she had to force
herself to walk, rather than run, up the stairs toward
her bedroom. If she didn't plan to make a fool of herself today, she had to stop reading something more into
everything that Mark said.

She passed Brooke in the hall.

"Hey." She stopped and squeezed the girl's shoulder.
"I haven't seen much of you this morning. You're moving kind of slowly. Are you feeling okay?"

"I'm fine." Brooke waved away her worry with a

brush of her hand before she tucked it in her pocket. "It's just a little headache."

"Well, you should rest for a while. You want to feel better so you can enjoy the dinner later."

"Oh, I'm better already." Crossing her arms, Brooke started down the hall. "Hey, don't we both have to get ready? You more than me. My mom won't be here until late this afternoon. After the family dinner with my aunts and uncles."

"Sorry your dad couldn't come."

Brooke paused and turned back to her. "It's okay. He's not ready. He just doesn't want to see me…like this." She patted her rounded stomach.

Shannon grimaced and then forced a smile. "Take it easy today."

Before Brooke could move again, Shannon crossed to her and gave her a warm hug. With a wave, she hurried to her own room, pulling the apron over her head as she went. She stood in front of the full-length mirror, pausing to study the woman looking back at her. She nodded in approval over the pretty black dress with its modest square neckline, a feminine silhouette and the perfect amount of swish at the hemline.

Although she'd only intended to run a comb through her hair, and maybe to plait it, she found herself blow-drying and heating up her curling iron. Where she usually didn't bother with makeup, she was suddenly applying mascara and a touch of lip gloss with a careful hand.

This was a special event. The house would be filled with dozens of guests. This was the first time she would spend a holiday with her son, as well. Any of those reasons could justify her desire to take extra care with her appearance today. They could even explain the nervous tension thrumming through her and keeping her distracted enough to boil the turkey and bake the cranberry sauce.

But to say that those factors were the only ones tripping up her steps today would be downright untrue, and she was tired. Of telling herself that Mark was just Blake's foster dad. Of reminding herself that she felt gratitude for Mark and nothing else. But most of all of lying to herself.

At ten minutes past one, forty-one people gathered around the two tables laden with more food than any group should eat in one day. Mark took his place in the center of one of the long tables, as four of the dads had been placed at the ends, two with the responsibility of cutting the twenty-five-pound turkeys.

"Are we going to eat soon? I'm starving," Blake said.

Mark turned to answer but realized that the boy wasn't speaking to him. Instead, he was carrying on an actual conversation with one of the girls, that younger one named Chelsea.

"I know," she said as she placed her napkin in her lap. "I'm hungry for two."

Blake blinked and lowered his gaze to the girl's tummy, as if just remembering why she was at Hope Haven. He cleared his throat. "I'll probably eat for four if no one stops me."

"You'd better wait until everyone's had seconds before you start making a pig of yourself," Mark said, entering the conversation as if he'd been invited.

"Don't worry, Trooper Mark," the girl assured him. "We'll have plenty of leftovers."

"Better not count on that," Blake said.

Mark slid a glance the boy's way, smiling. Blake

might not have the whole boy-girl thing down yet, but he was trying awfully hard to make this one laugh. He couldn't blame the kid for trying. Chelsea was an attractive young woman, and about Blake's age. He just hoped the boy wasn't reading more into the polite dinner conversation than what was there. That would be a mistake, and Mark was making enough of those for the both of them.

"Where are your parents?" Blake asked the girl in a low voice.

"Remember, I said they couldn't make it."

"But didn't you say you were from Keego Harbor?"

"They had some family thing."

Just then Shannon stepped to her place across the table from Blake, and instead of sitting, she rested her hands on the back of the chair.

"Thanks to all of you for joining us and for bringing such lovely dishes to share. As has become our tradition at the Hope Haven Thanksgiving celebration, before we give thanks to God for our food, we take turns sharing something that we are thankful for. Would anyone like to start?"

She scanned the length of one table and then, smiling, traveled the other one with her gaze. She'd spoken of holiday traditions at Hope Haven, but she hadn't mentioned the reality that a whole new group of residents and their families came each year to observe those traditions. A new group would show up to do the same thing next year. And another the year after that, if the Hope Haven house managed to keep standing that long.

"Now, don't everyone jump at once," Shannon prompted again.

"I'll go," came a small voice from the other table.

The exotic-looking young girl he'd met in the basement yesterday came to her feet.

"Thanks for stepping up, Kelly," Shannon said.

The girl only grinned. "I'm thankful to have my mother here with me for Thanksgiving. She drove all the way from Cincinnati just to be with us."

Shannon winced, probably in honor of the girls whose parents lived closer and yet couldn't fit the event into their schedules. "That's great, Kelly. Anything else?"

"I'm thankful for everyone here and for learning to make a pumpkin pie yesterday, because I'll probably eat mine all by myself."

Kelly's comment drew a laugh, and Shannon continued to the next person at the far table. Some parents expressed gratitude for their daughters not losing their faith during these difficult times. A few parents and kids repeated the sentiments that they were blessed to have their families and friends.

"I'm thankful for Hope Haven because it provides a place for the girls to go where they can be… comfortable," one of the dads said.

Blake stiffened next to him, and Mark reached over and squeezed his elbow. Mark couldn't help wanting to ask the guy whose comfort he was talking about, his and his wife's or their daughter's. For the first time, he had a sense of the painful alienation Shannon must have experienced while she was pregnant with Blake. He caught her gaze for a fraction of a second, but she only chewed the corner of her lip and glanced away.

The process continued with no more unsettling comments, and the redhead seated next to Shannon started first on the second table.

"Giving thanks that God made pregnancy last only

forty weeks instead of sixty," another girl added for a laugh.

"Thank you, Brooke." Shannon's gaze lingered on the girl longer than on the others, but then she moved on.

Soon it was Mark's turn, and he scrambled for the right words. "I'm thankful for everyone who came here to support all of these young people," he said in an attempt to include Blake. He forced himself not to say something about those in obvious absence.

After a sharp glance his way, Shannon looked to Blake.

He picked at his cuticles, not looking up from the table. "Um, I guess what I'm really thankful for is all of this food."

The laughter around the tables seemed to surprise him.

"Well, at least he's honest," one of the other parents noted, drawing another laugh.

If he hadn't been watching, Mark might have missed the disappointment in Shannon's eyes. It was there, and then it was gone. Clearly, she'd hoped for something more from her son. A few days ago Mark would have told her she was expecting too much from a teenage boy or even that she had no right to expect anything at all. Now, though, he was grateful for the table separating them. If not for it, he probably would have pulled her into his arms and told her that everything was going to be okay between her and Blake. How could he promise something like that when he knew from experience that there were no guarantees in life?

Around the table, the guests recounted their blessings, and finally it was Shannon's turn.

"I am thankful for the opportunity to get to know

each of your daughters," she said without qualifying it by saying "under the circumstances." "They have been such blessings to my life, and I have learned so much from them. I also wanted to say that I am grateful this Thanksgiving for the opportunity to get to know my son, Blake, whom I placed for adoption when I was a teenager."

She gestured to the boy, who was still staring at his plate, and seemed to wait for some response from the other guests, but their lack of reaction suggested this was already old news, even to the parents.

Shannon cleared her throat. "And I'm also thankful for Trooper Mark Shoffner, who opened his home and his life to Blake as a foster parent. If that wasn't enough, he and Blake have been doing volunteer work to help make much-needed improvements at Hope Haven."

She waited for the polite applause to die down before continuing, but instead of addressing the crowd as she'd done before, she focused in on Mark. "I appreciate your help. Thank you for giving me the opportunity to get to know...my son."

Her voice broke at the last two words, and a lump the size of one of those sweet potatoes in front of him formed inside his throat. He caught her eye just in time to see her brush a tear off her cheek.

"Now everyone please stand for our Thanksgiving prayer."

She reached for the hands of the girls sitting on either side of her and waited for the rest of the guests to join hands. Mark took hold of Blake's work-roughened hand and that of the mother seated on his opposite side. How inappropriate it was that while they were preparing to give thanks, all he could think about was what the skin of Shannon's hand would feel like if he'd been sitting next to her instead.

"Father, we come to You today to give thanks for the many blessings You have bestowed on each one of us," Shannon prayed. "Thank You for this food and for the hands that prepared it. Thank You for safe travel for all of our guests. Lead us to be Your heart and hands in our world. In Jesus' name. Amen."

Immediately, the room was filled with the chatter of dozens of conversations and the sounds of platters and serving dishes being passed from hand to hand. Blake ladled a little of everything on his plate, except the sliced tomatoes. He managed not to make too much of a pig of himself, though he wasn't shy when Shannon asked if anyone wanted seconds. On the other hand, Chelsea, who'd said she was starving, ate no more than a serving of turkey and a dinner roll, claiming heartburn.

Between bites of mashed potatoes and turkey with cranberry sauce, Mark studied his fellow guests. A few of the moms sat doting on their pregnant daughters, while at least one dad appeared ready to bolt from the scene at any moment. A pair of little girls from two different families had already made friends in this party for their older sisters. A little boy crouched low in his seat, clearly miserable in his dress-up clothes.

It was strange for Mark to think that he shared something in common with each of these girls. With Shannon, as well. All of them had disappointed their parents with their actions, and all of them would live with the consequences of their mistakes for years to come. Would they feel like he did sometimes that his family had made up their minds about him and there was nothing he could do to change them?

The eating had begun to slow, with conversations

filling the void, when Shannon stood up again. "Okay, girls, it's time for dessert."

At once, all twelve girls rose from their seats and started toward the kitchen, some moving slowly, carefully, with their hands pressed to their lower backs.

"Now, as we mentioned earlier, the girls had a lesson in pumpkin-pie baking last night. Each one has made a pie from scratch, including crust, so we hope you all will enjoy dessert, courtesy of these daughters, sisters and friends." Shannon smiled at the families and then glanced back at the swinging kitchen door. "Don't forget the homemade whipping cream, girls."

Mark couldn't help but grin at her enthusiasm. She'd made a holiday that could have been lonely and bitter for the residents into a true celebration and probably softened some strained relationships at the same time.

"The girls will also be bringing out some brownies." She looked over her shoulder at the closed door. "It's taking longer than expected to cut the pies. Maybe I should have told them they didn't all have to use the same knife."

As she stood there a few moments longer, soft murmurs around her slowly unfurled into louder questions. "I think I'll check on the progress in there," she said finally.

Shannon had only taken a few steps toward the kitchen when an anguished cry came from the other side of the door.

Kelly pushed the door open. "Miss Shannon! It's Brooke. We need help in here."

Shannon kicked off her shoes and ran.

Chapter Ten

"I'm here, Brooke," Shannon announced as she charged through the door.

The girls were crowded around Brooke, their voices sharp and discordant, their pies lined up on the counter, forgotten. Shannon had to squeeze through them to get to the center of the circle.

"Oh, Brooke, honey." She brushed back the girl's hair.

"I knew there was something wrong. I *knew* it."

Brooke just continued rocking in her curled position, her hands gripping the ball of her stomach. Shannon hadn't heard him come in behind her, but Mark was suddenly in the room with them, working his way through the crowd.

"Girls, could you do us a favor and go handle the guests out there?" he asked. "Miss Shannon and I are going to help Brooke."

They waited for Shannon's nod and filed from the room.

"Is she in labor?" he asked as soon as the door closed. "How many weeks is she? How far apart are her contractions?"

Shannon was so focused on Brooke that his questions barely registered. "It's too soon." She continued stroking the girl's arm. "I should have done something. I should have—"

"Listen to me, Shannon." Mark rested a hand on her shoulder. "I need to know how far along she is in case I have to deliver the baby."

It must have been the word *deliver* that broke through her haze. She blinked and then shook her head. Of course, Mark would have had training in case he had to attend an emergency delivery. "No, she *shouldn't* deliver. She's just thirty-four weeks."

He kneeled and took Brooke's wrist to get a pulse. Her hands were warm and red, and perspiration dotted her face. "Brooke, can you tell me what's going on?"

"I hurt," she whined.

"I know you do, kiddo. Do you know how far apart your contractions are?"

"Don't know." She winced as if the pain was taking hold again. "It's not just my stomach. My head is killing me, and I feel nauseated."

"Could be preeclampsia." Shannon wasn't even sure she'd spoken those words aloud until Mark straightened.

"I'll call 9-1-1," he said.

"No. I'll take her. It will be faster than waiting for the ambulance."

"Let me," he insisted. "I can make it there faster than you can, and I can get a patrol-car escort if necessary."

Her mouth opened, probably to say no again, but then she closed her lips and nodded. "I'm coming, too."

"Fine. Now, Brooke, I'm going to be as careful as I can, but I need to lift you so we can get you to the hospital." He slipped his hands behind her back and knees.

Immediately, tears started draining from Brooke's eyes. "I want my mom."

Shannon stood and wiped away some of the tears making trails down the girl's face. "I know you do. I'll call her so she can meet us at the hospital instead of coming here."

"I didn't mean to ruin your party," Brooke said.

"You didn't ruin anything, sweetie." Again Shannon brushed the girl's hair back from her face. "Let's just focus on making sure that you and the baby are okay."

Brooke closed her eyes and spoke in a low voice. "Me and Parasite."

"Parasite?" Mark mouthed.

"The baby," Shannon whispered. "I'll get Blake."

She called for him out in the cafeteria area, and instead of balking as she thought he might, he hurried into the kitchen. She collected their coats from the closet and the emergency information card she kept in an index card box. She stretched Brooke's coat over the front of her, and Blake held the door open for all of them.

After a brief trip back to the dining area to tell everyone to finish their dinner and to pray for Brooke and her baby, she caught up with them at the truck. Mark had already stretched the girl across the backseat and had Blake sitting back there with her, holding her head on a makeshift pillow of their coats.

Mark took off so quickly that gravel spit up behind them. Even at that pace, the drive to the hospital in Novi took too long, allowing her memories to find purchase in today's crisis when they should have remained banished to the past. No matter how hard she tried to squash them, those recollections clung to her like the last icicles on a roof covered in melting snow.

How could she be so selfish? Brooke's life and the

life of her child might be in danger. The least she could do would be to give the girl her full attention.

"Is she going to be okay?" Blake whispered.

Shannon whipped her head to the side to see if Brooke had fallen asleep, but the girl's eyes fluttered open.

"Yeah, am I? And what about my baby?"

"Everything's going to be fine," Shannon promised, though she knew better than to promise anything when she might not be able to deliver.

What *could* she do for her? How could she help her if Brooke lost the baby? Yes, the girl had planned to place her child for adoption, but she might face unimaginable guilt if the baby didn't survive. Shannon felt so powerless, impotent, just when Brooke needed something that would give her hope. Well, she might not have anything to offer her, but she knew someone who did.

"Father, I'm entrusting Brooke and her baby to You." She whispered the prayer with her eyes open so she could continue watching the girl.

As they pulled into the hospital plaza and the big emergency sign came into view, Shannon released a breath that she hadn't even known she was holding. They would be fine now; they were in the capable hands of medical professionals. And more than that, God would hold them in the palm of His always-sufficient hand. Maybe it was selfish of her, but she prayed He would hold on extratight.

Mark sneaked a peek at the woman who'd recently taken up residence next to him in one of those cloth waiting room chairs that might as well have been made of stone. Shannon still blamed herself for everything that had happened. She'd refused to leave Brooke's bedside since they'd arrived at the hospital, and now that she'd been displaced by Brooke's mother in her vigil, she didn't seem to know what to do with herself.

Whether she realized it or not, Blake had been watching her as well ever since she'd returned to the waiting room. He'd turned back to the television when Mark had caught him doing it.

"Do you want to go back to Hope Haven?" Mark asked her.

For a few seconds, Shannon said nothing, but then she startled as if she'd only then noticed that someone was speaking to her.

"What? Uh…maybe we should wait a little longer to see if the doctors can help her."

He understood that by "help her" Shannon meant to stop Brooke's labor. He'd prayed for the same thing. As if it wasn't difficult enough for a teen having a baby when she was still a kid herself, giving birth to a preemie would make her situation even more challenging.

"Her mom's here with her now."

"I know. It's just…" She let her words trail away without ever saying what it *just* was.

"You're going to have to leave here sometime," he said gently. "You still have all of those people back at Hope Haven."

An expression of misery covered her features. "But not yet, okay? I just can't leave her."

"Okay."

Just then a group of adults and Hope Haven residents entered through the sliding glass door into the already full emergency waiting room. Other visitors, all with their own holiday crises to contend with, stared at the gaggle of pregnant teens. If the girls were aware that they'd become an object of curiosity, they pretended not to notice.

A redhead named Holly hurried their way. "Any word?"

"Only that the doctors are trying to stop her labor," Shannon answered, shaking her head as she said it.

"She's going to be all right," Holly assured her. "We've all been praying."

Shannon nodded, her eyes too bright. Obviously, the girl hadn't lived long enough to know that even God sometimes said no, but Mark had to appreciate the way she'd tried to cheer up Shannon.

"Is it okay if Blake comes with us to the cafeteria for some ice cream?"

Holly had addressed the question to Shannon instead of him, which at any other time would have made her happy. But she didn't notice that the girl had spoken to her, so Mark turned to Blake himself.

"Hey, would you like to go to the cafeteria with these young ladies?"

Blake looked up as if surprised to see the girls and their parents there, though he hadn't turned a page of the *Sports Illustrated* issue he'd been reading for more than an hour. He scanned the girls' faces and then looked at the door as if he was disappointed that one of them was missing. Finally, he nodded.

"Want me to bring you anything?"

Mark shook his head. "We'll be fine with vending machine fare."

He wasn't sure why he'd said they would be fine with anything. Shannon didn't answer at all. She wasn't fine right now and likely wouldn't be better after consuming tiny packages of cheese curls or a chocolate bar.

After they were gone, he turned in his seat so that

his right knee came up on the cushion, and he watched her. After what seemed like several minutes, she looked at him. Her gaze narrowed.

"What?"

"Let's take a walk." Mark indicated the doors that separated the emergency department from the other parts of the hospital.

"I don't know." She was already shaking her head. "I should be here in case they have any news."

"We'll go just here in the hospital. You have your cell. And everyone has your number, right?" He waited for her nod before continuing. "If they don't see us in here, they'll call you. Or text. Don't worry."

She glanced with uncertainty toward another set of doors through which they'd taken Brooke when they'd first arrived, but when Mark stood, Shannon came to her feet, as well.

"Maybe it would do me good to move around and stretch out a bit."

She followed a few steps behind as he took several turns through the maze of hospital hallways. He stopped in a narrow hall filled with offices. It appeared to be deserted for the holiday. He leaned a shoulder against the wall, and she did the same, facing him.

"Can you tell me what's wrong? I mean, other than what's happening with Brooke."

From her body language—tight and stiff—he was certain that there was something. He had some suspicions about what at least part of it was. He just didn't know for certain.

"I should be able to recognize the signs of problems. How could I have missed this?"

"Brooke told you that she'd tried to cover up her symptoms so she wouldn't mess up the celebration. She even said her face was swollen this morning, so she stayed in her room until the swelling went down. That's a huge symptom of preeclampsia, isn't it?"

She nodded. "I just don't understand it. How could she not know how dangerous that was or that she and her baby are far more important to me than any celebration?"

"I'm sure she knew that. But whether she's about to become a mother or not, she's still just a kid. She probably hadn't had a lot to look forward to lately, and, as she said, she didn't want to ruin the party."

She accepted his explanation with a nod, but she didn't seem to believe him. That she'd crossed her arms tightly over her chest as if those were the only things holding her together told him there was more to the story.

"Come on, Shannon. This isn't only about you blaming yourself, or even your worries about Brooke." He paused until she finally looked over at him. "The births are really tough for you, aren't they?"

Her eyes widened. Was she really so surprised that he would understand her? That each birth would scratch at old scars, rewounding. He knew as much as anyone about wounds that scabbed over but never really healed.

A faraway look came into her eyes, and he could only wait through the long pause for her to finally open up to him. "It's like repeating the most awful day of my life again and again, each time with slightly different details but the same ending. Brooke's story is especially hard because I had complications with my pregnancy, too, and Blake had to be delivered by emergency C-section." She blinked her eyes several times, as if to push away images flicking through her thoughts.

"The stories aren't all the same, are they?" he asked. "Some of the girls keep their babies."

She nodded. "Sure. A few. But the stories are similar in that another child has become a mother, and no matter what she chooses to do from that point on, nothing can change that."

"I don't know how you handled it when the girls didn't know about Blake. How could you hold your story in like that?" It surprised him now how easily that rolled off his tongue. He'd not only fully accepted that she was Blake's mother, without proof, but he'd also no longer questioned whether she could commit to a relationship with her son.

She shrugged, her lips forming a sad smile. "I just tried to share in their joys. Who couldn't find joy in the birth of a new baby? When there were tears as they said goodbye to their newborns, I could empathize and sympathize more than they knew. Even the ones who had to welcome their babies without the birth fathers, I could relate to that pain, too."

"Are you ever going to tell me about *him?*"

"Blake's father?"

He nodded. She studied him with a narrowed gaze. "I just don't understand why it matters so much for you to know about him. I get why Blake would want to know. But why you?"

"Just curious."

More curious than he'd had any right to be. He simply *had* to know. He had no claim to her, but he couldn't bear the thought of a man who'd touched her and then left her to face the consequence of his child alone. With those feelings so entwined, Mark couldn't decide whether he was being more protective of her, or just jealous.

She'd demurred again, and he sensed that she would never tell her whole story to him or to Blake. So it surprised him when she started talking again.

"I used to work so hard to meet my parents' impossible expectations. I would jump through every hoop they set out for me, and they set out more hoops than circus lion tamers. It was never enough."

He opened his mouth to object. He'd heard this part of the story before. Now he wanted to hear the part she didn't want to tell.

But she shook her head to stop him. "And then I met Scott. He seemed to accept me just the way I was. Combine that with his irresistible bad-boy image, and I was a goner."

"An easy mark?" he couldn't help asking. That he bristled over his own words was telling. Just the thought of someone taking advantage of her vulnerability infuriated him.

She lifted a brow, making him worry that she would stop telling her story, but then she nodded. "I guess I was. Do you know how appealing it can be to have someone love you for you, even if that person is only pretending?"

This time he nodded. As a matter of fact, he did know what that was like. At first, Kim had seemed so impressed with his dedication to his work, with his determination to serve the public with honor, but then she'd used the thing she was supposed to love about him as her excuse to betray him. He blinked, pushing away the memory. This wasn't the time for his story when Shannon was finally ready to tell hers.

"I knew my parents would never approve of him, so the only way I could continue seeing him was to keep him a secret. And the only way I could keep Scott, or at least so I thought, was to do things that I knew were wrong."

Mark cleared his throat. "You don't have to tell me more if you don't want to."

He'd had an almost compulsive need to hear details about the guy who'd left her, and now all he wanted her to do was to stop.

"And then I told him I was pregnant. At first, I kept it a secret from everyone. Him included. I couldn't even admit it to myself. When I finally did tell him, I was already having terrible morning sickness, and I'd resorted to stretch pants. And you want to know what he did?"

No, he didn't want to know, but like a driver at a grisly accident scene, he couldn't resist a "look" into her past. He nodded.

"He left. In every possible way." She squeezed her eyes shut, and when she opened them, they were damp. "At first, he said the kid probably wasn't his. Then he said he didn't care if it was. And, finally, he drove off, leaving me sitting on top of a picnic table at a park about three miles from my house."

The fury that filled him was as intense as it was surprising. He had to force his hands not to fist with the need to strike out at her past. Instead, he crossed his arms in front of him. "What did you do?"

Sometime during her story they must have shifted because now, instead of both of them leaning an arm against the corridor wall as they faced each other, she stood with both shoulder blades on the wall and he stood out in front of her. She stared at the floor, looking as vulnerable as she must have back then.

"I had to call my parents at one o'clock in the morning. I was crying so hard that they could barely understand me. They were furious that I had sneaked out of the house, but I told them that was the least of their worries."

Her story was distressing on so many levels, but one part kept repeating in his thoughts. Festering. The kid had taken her heart, her innocence and her trust in people and tossed them away like fast-food wrappers. And he'd left her to face the consequences of their actions. Alone.

"He should never have left you."

Until she glanced up, he didn't realize he'd spoken those words aloud. He should have stopped there, could have held on to that final remnant of distance to which he'd been clinging. But he couldn't. Not this time.

Before he could stop himself, before sanity and discretion could catch him in their safety net, he spoke the words that would change everything. "I never would have left you."

Those lovely eyes widened, as if she knew what he was about to do, even before he did. She froze, appearing unsure, but she didn't look away. She simply watched him and waited. Her uncertainty was his undoing.

It wasn't a huge distance—only a little more than two feet separated them—but he bridged it with one step and then dipped his head and brushed his lips over hers. He'd imagined them more times than he should have, obsessed about them when he should have been strongly rejecting their appeal, but the feel of her lips against his still surprised him. So smooth and pillow soft.

It was the briefest of kisses, just a breath of a caress, barely long enough for her eyes to flutter closed. Yet Mark recognized his mistake the moment he eased away from her, his sharp intake of breath drawing in her essence. He'd been kissed before. He'd been *mar-*

ried before. But this was different. As dangerous as it
was warm and comforting. For from the moment her
eyes opened and she stared up at him in confusion, all
he could think about was kissing her again.

It was a bad idea, and he knew it. Once was difficult enough to recover from, difficult enough to redi-
rect his thoughts back to Blake, where they belonged.
But to kiss her again, to think it through first and still
come to the same conclusion? There would be no back-
tracking from that. Whether he was ready to or not, he
would be forced to admit that his feelings for Shannon
were very real.

Even as he reasoned and attempted to dissuade his
actions, his head bent to hers again. Just as their lips
touched, Shannon's phone beeped, and they jerked back
as if they'd both touched a flame and had been caught
with their fingers burning. They had…and they had.

Shannon rubbed the place where her head had hit
the wall and then pulled her phone from the outside
compartment of her purse. She fumbled through a
few screens and opened the text. Because she held the
phone out from her, he was able to read the words from
Brooke's mother as she did.

Miss Shannon, where are you? Can you return to the
waiting room? Carla.

Without looking at him, Shannon jogged down the
hall. Mark hurried after her, his thoughts spinning
with the events that had just taken place between them.
When she made a quick left turn, he called out to her.

"Wait. Shannon."

She stopped but still didn't look back at him.

"It's the other way."

Her shoulders shifted, but she did an about-face and ran right past him, her gaze brushing his as she passed. He continued to follow, matching her pace but purposely staying behind her. When they reached the waiting room, she hurried over to the girl's mom, who sat with her face buried in her hands. A lump formed in Mark's throat before Shannon even sat next to the woman and wrapped an arm around her.

The woman stared straight ahead but appeared to see nothing. "Brooke. She...wants—"

Her voice broke off then in a sob, but Mark continued to watch her, trying to understand the woman's message from her few words and her defeated body language. *Wants?* He tried to decipher the comment. Brooke was at least strong enough to want to something. That was good, right? But what had happened to the baby?

"What is it, Carla?" Shannon prompted. "Tell us."

As the woman turned to face Shannon, her eyes filled again. "She wants...to keep the baby."

Shannon let out a long breath. Mark could certainly relate to that. He'd nearly had a heart attack himself as the idea of kids having kids escalated to the prospect of some of them dying in the process. Obviously, Shannon had a lot on her plate right now, beyond attempting to build a relationship with her son, which itself was no small matter.

He shouldn't have added to the complicated mix of her life by kissing her, but even now he couldn't force himself to be sorry. As much as they needed to discuss what had happened tonight, what had been happening between them for days, now wasn't the time. But they would talk about it, after this crisis had passed, after some of the details regarding Blake's future were in place, after Mark had taken the time to sort out his feelings, as well. They needed to talk about it, make sense of it, determine what it meant. Not now. But soon.

Chapter Eleven

Shannon rubbed small circles on the back of the over-whelmed mother seated next to her. She could relate to the rush of feelings Brooke's mother must have been experiencing. She was a bit overwrought herself. All of her senses were on high alert, every sound clanging and harsh, every light glaring. Her lips still tingled even now with what felt like aftershocks of a high-magnitude earthquake though the kiss had been gentle and sweet.

But she didn't have the luxury of time for thinking about Mark and the feelings his kiss had awakened. Or even any free time to worry that the thoughts she was having about Mark somehow betrayed Blake.

"It's going to be okay," she crooned, continuing to rub Carla's back.

The woman's shoulders heaved with the violence of her sobs. Shannon was tempted to tell her that the situation could be so much worse than Brooke changing her mind about adoption. That there were health issues and even lives in the balance. But if Brooke's mother had been thinking clearly, she would have realized that.

On the opposite side of the room, Shannon caught sight of Mark, where he'd settled after Carla had made

her announcement. She appreciated that he was trying to give the two of them space but wondered if he
needed a buffer, as well. After a few minutes, the woman's sobs slowed.

"Now, can you tell me what the doctor said?"

Carla squeezed her eyes shut and then opened them
again. "They're giving Brooke medication to mature
the baby's lungs because they're not going to be able
to stop her labor. The only way for Brooke to get better is for them to deliver the baby."

"At least they have a plan going forward."

"Brooke does, anyway," Carla said with a sigh. "She
said she's changed her mind. She wants—"

"To keep the baby," Shannon finished for her, nod-
ding. "You already shared that with us."

Carla rested her elbows on her knees and her chin
in the V formed where her wrists touched. "What am
I going to do?"

"Come on, sweetie. You know what you're going to
do." Shannon reached over to pat her shoulder. "You're
going to support your daughter in the same way you've
supported her every minute since she told you she was
pregnant. Every minute since she was a little girl with
a scraped knee."

"But how can I support…this?"

Shannon didn't miss the mother's meaning. It was
so much easier to get behind her daughter's decision
when it didn't mean causing more upheaval and finan-
cial strain by bringing the baby into their home and
lives. Not to mention the humiliation of having all of the
neighbors know the truth. But Shannon couldn't allow
her resentment over the mother's reaction to keep her
from helping this family that would need her support
more than ever.

"I understand that it's hard," she began. "But please try to respect Brooke's decision. Whether she chooses to place her child with a loving family or to raise the baby herself, she will always have to live with that decision. Believe me, I know. So it has to be the right choice for her. And, as her mother, you'll have to live with however you choose to respond to her decision."

Suddenly, Carla's eyes widened. "But this baby will be a preemie. He or she might not even survive. How will Brooke bear it if she has just decided to mother this child, and then she has to bury her baby?"

"Try to have faith."

She blinked. "What?"

"You believe that God is capable of healing, right?"

"Of course I do." Carla appeared anything but sure.

"Then you have to trust Him to do it here. Your daughter and your grandchild will need your support, but right now more than anything they need your prayers."

Carla could only nod as her eyes filled with tears once more, so Shannon gathered her in her arms for a long hug. Finally, Carla pulled back from her.

"I need to get back in there to Brooke."

Only after the woman disappeared through the door leading deeper into the emergency department did Shannon notice that Mark hadn't been the only witness to their conversation; Blake was there, too. She wasn't sure when he'd returned from the cafeteria, but he sat next to Mark, watching her with wide eyes. He didn't look away when he realized she'd caught him watching, either.

How much of their conversation had he overheard? Had he been there for the part about young mothers living with the consequences of their choices? Was Blake beginning to understand her own painful decision to place him for adoption? If he did understand, did that mean he would finally forgive her? Maybe Blake would give her the chance to build a relationship with him after all. Maybe she would have the chance to be the kind of mother to him that she always should have been.

After several seconds, longer than he was usually able to maintain eye contact, Blake lowered his gaze to his hands in his lap, making a project of entwining his fingers in several different formations. But the man sitting next to him was still there, as if waiting for his turn to receive Shannon's notice. Didn't he know she couldn't ignore him if she tried? He watched her for a long time, and then he smiled, his approval warming her as much as his gaze.

Funny thing about hope, it was contagious. If there were possibilities for a relationship between her and Blake, could she and Mark have a chance, as well? Despite the unlikely way they'd met, despite that trusting a man seemed impossibly hard to her, despite everything, she was tempted to open herself to the possibility. Maybe. Just maybe.

Hope was contagious, all right. She just worried it was dangerous, as well.

The final minutes of the holiday had slipped away by the time that Mark's truck rolled up Hope Haven's driveway, the gravel crunching too loudly beneath its tires. The line of cars that had filled the long drive earlier had been whittled to two. As he parked, Mark glanced in the rearview mirror, expecting Blake to have already crashed in the backseat. Instead, the boy sat up straight and was staring back at him in the glass.

"Is she… I mean, are *they* going to be okay?"

"Well, the doctor said the longer they can delay her delivery, the more they can develop the baby's lungs and the better chance for a positive outcome," Mark said, repeating some of the words he'd heard outside of Brooke's hospital room.

"Sounds like a nonanswer to me," Blake grumbled.

"Yeah, I guess it does." Mark chuckled.

"They just don't know what to say." Shannon shifted to sit sideways in the front passenger seat. "Brooke and the baby will be fine. They *have* to be."

"How do you know that for sure?" Blake asked.

For a long time, she said nothing, but then she shook her head. "There's no way to know that for sure. I just have to believe it."

Blake sighed. "Somebody's finally telling the truth."

"That's not the whole truth, Blake," Shannon said. "The doctor told us to go home since all we could do tonight was wait and hope for a healthy delivery. But she was wrong. We can do more than that. We can pray."

"You're right," Mark agreed. "We can do that."

He had to admire her confidence. She'd been a rock during this whole ordeal, whether she realized it or not. She'd supported Brooke until her mother had arrived and then had bolstered the girl's mother, offering a loving demonstration for Blake at the same time. For him, too.

"Is it okay if we pray *and* get some sleep?" Blake asked with a yawn. "Not necessarily in that order."

The adults laughed.

"He's right. I'd better get inside. The other girls are still pretty upset." She sighed. "They're worried they'll develop complications like Brooke did."

"Does that happen often?" Mark asked to stall her.

"Teen moms are more likely to have premature deliveries than other mothers, and there can always be complications in pregnancy. But we do everything we can here to decrease the risk by giving the girls good prenatal care. I'll see you guys tomorrow."

"Maybe it will finally be dry enough for us to fix those gutters," Mark said.

She nodded. "And then maybe you could take a look at the roof over the porch where it always leaks."

"That chores list sure keeps growing."

Chuckling, she pressed her fingertips to her lips. "Our offers of help around here are few and far between."

"I see."

"Well…" She placed her hand on the door handle.

"Wait." He didn't want her to go. Even if he hadn't had the chance to be alone with her again to find out if that kiss had meant anything to her, too, at least they'd shared the same space for the past several hours. He searched for another way to stall, but there wasn't anything left to say to keep her there.

"Here, let me get that for you," he said finally.

He rounded the truck and opened the door for her, allowing light to flood into the cab. As she twisted to climb out, shadows of exhaustion under her eyes became apparent. With a glance toward Blake, who'd already settled into the backseat and had closed his eyes, Mark reached out to help her down to the running board. She stared at his outstretched hand for several seconds and then rested her hand in it, so small and soft when compared to his own. After she'd descended the step to the ground, the touch lingered, as intimate as a kiss. A promise made without words. Did she feel it, too?

"Good night, Miss Shannon," came a sleepy murmur from the backseat.

They jumped, jerking their hands back and looking inside the still-open door. Blake's eyes were closed just as they'd been before. They exchanged a secret smile and closed the door, the truck's interior light flicking off, leaving only a subtle glow coming from the back porch and barn lights.

Blake had called her Miss Shannon like the Hope Haven residents did, but it surprised Mark how much he wished the boy had called her Mom instead. Where in the beginning it had been so easy for him to blame her for deserting her child, now he saw the selflessness of her act. Even as a child herself and even at the expense of her own happiness, she'd tried to do what was best for her son.

She cleared her throat. "Well, good night."

"Good night."

She shivered, making him aware that the wind had picked up. The scent of the air had changed to a tangy crispness, as if the rain they'd endured all week was but a precursor to snow. With a wave, she trudged toward the house.

"Shannon," he called after her.

She stopped, pausing for a few heartbeats before looking back over her shoulder. Was she bracing herself for whatever he had to say?

"At some point, we're going to have to talk about what happened today." He would have said "the kiss," but he could tell from her wide eyes that she knew what he'd meant.

"I know." And then she smiled.

It was all Mark could do not to stalk across the yard and take her in his arms right then and there. The very thing he shouldn't have done the first time. The timing couldn't have been worse, and he knew it. His wounds from being burned in his marriage were still fresh, the skin grafts covering them just beginning to take. And Shannon was in no position to be even considering romance now, either—not with Blake just reentering her life and seesawing before her between stranger and son.

He should step back from her for both of their sakes, but he couldn't do it. From that first day when she'd needed him to step up for her son, Shannon had drawn him to her. She'd effortlessly unlocked the dead bolt he'd set over his heart, and now he was perilously close to allowing her to make a home for herself there, complete with wind chimes and a welcome mat.

No, now wasn't the perfect time. But after the legal matters regarding Blake's custody were settled, after the boy he'd promised to care for was comfortable in his new life, then just maybe he would be ready to take the risk of loving Shannon.

"The praise service was great, wasn't it?" Shannon asked over her shoulder as they passed through the sliding-door entrance of the unfamiliar hospital Sunday afternoon.

"As good as any church service in a house could be, I guess," Blake said.

Trailing behind them through the door, Mark chuckled. "So you're a huge fan of services in regular church buildings, then?"

Blake made a noncommittal sound, but Shannon didn't buy it. His eyes had been as damp as anyone's at the praise service where they'd celebrated the healthy delivery of Brooke's baby girl and Brooke's improving health.

"I don't know about you guys, but I thought it was amazing." She frowned at them over her shoulder as they passed a gift shop and large waiting room, but she was too happy to hold the expression. "Such a great way to end Thanksgiving weekend. We had so much more to be thankful for than we ever knew at dinner on Thursday."

"Yes, more than we knew," Mark agreed.

Shannon swallowed, her pulse picking up as layers of possible meaning in his words enfolded her like a hug. She forced herself to look at the signs leading to the pediatric intensive care unit, trying not to read too much into his words. But since she'd overanalyzed every conversation they'd had, every unintentional look, each accidental touch in the past three days, she didn't expect now to be any different. Before, she'd given herself the excuse that they'd all had too much time to think while they waited and prayed for the safe delivery of Brooke's baby, so what was her excuse now?

Mark had seemed to have no trouble keeping his thoughts on the tasks at hand while he and Blake completed several outdoor projects at Hope Haven before Blake had to start at his new school and Mark had to return to work. What if the kiss she and Mark had shared had been just a kiss to him, a momentary lapse in judgment, while it had meant everything to her?

Was this what love felt like? This feeling of walking a tightrope in heels, with neither a pole for balance nor a safety net to protect against tragedy. She wasn't certain, but the one thing she did know for sure was that those feelings she'd once had for Scott hadn't been love at all. Not like this. Still, this wasn't the first time she'd mistaken a guy's motives. Mark knew her history, knew her weaknesses. Had he, for some reason she would never understand, used that knowledge against her?

"Why is the baby in a different hospital than Brooke?" Blake asked as they rounded yet another corner in the maze of halls.

"She needs to be in a hospital with a pediatric ICU for a while so the doctors had to transfer her," Shannon explained.

"But Brooke's still in the other hospital. Who's going to be with the baby?"

"A lot of times when a baby has to be transferred to a hospital with a pediatric ICU, the father will be the one to visit until the mother can be released from the other hospital, and they can come together."

"But not girls like her," Blake grumbled.

"No. The dads aren't often in the picture."

She sensed both Mark and Blake watching her and waiting for her to add "like yours," but she didn't bother. They all knew that story now in varying levels of detail. There was no need for her to berate a guy who'd never been there and would never be there. Some things just were what they were.

"Don't worry. She'll be at the hospital as soon as she can be."

With one last turn, they approached the ICU nursery. It had a limited viewing space, and even most of those windows were shaded by miniblinds.

"Which one do you think is Lilly Ann?" Blake peeked through a small area of open blinds at several incubators. Their tiny, struggling occupants rested under different types of lights, machines and monitors attached with cords to their tiny arms, noses, heads and feet.

Shannon and Mark exchanged a grin over Blake's

use of the name Brooke had given her baby. Again, electricity flickered, at least on her end.

Mark squeezed in, bumping Blake with his shoulder. "If I were to guess, I would say she's the one with Brooke's mom sitting next to her."

Sure enough, the girl's mother wore a sterile gown and sat next to a baby with a little pink cap and a diaper. Not in an incubator but on a tray of sorts, the baby looked as if she was getting a suntan under a warming light.

"She's so much bigger than the other babies in there," Blake pointed out, indicating several small, frail infants, some with deep red skin, some appearing to struggle for each breath.

Shannon nodded. "At thirty-four weeks and almost five pounds, she's what they call 'late preterm.' She's not expected to be in the pediatric ICU for very long."

Those other sweet babies across the room drew her attention. Many would face more significant challenges in the weeks and months to come than any of them could imagine. She whispered a prayer for them and their parents.

Just as her eyes opened, a nurse exited through the nursery door, and the melody of a lullaby followed her. From the way her mouth was moving, Carla appeared to be the one singing to the baby next to her. She must have sensed that someone was watching because she looked up and smiled when she recognized them. Crossing to the window, she opened the blinds wider so they could get a better look and then returned to her seat. She pointed to the preemie next to her and mouthed the words, "That's my grandbaby."

A lump wedged itself in Shannon's throat, and her eyes felt damp. Brooke's mother was supporting her daughter's decision after all. She prayed that the teen's father would get behind her, as well. The family had a long road ahead of them, but she just knew that with hard work and a lot of prayer, they would be all right.

"You did a good thing."

The sound of Mark's voice called her back from her musings, and she turned to him, lifting an eyebrow.

"We heard what you said to Brooke's mom."

"I didn't do anything," she said, as flustered by his approval as she was flattered by it. She sneaked a peek at Blake, unsure whether he was listening. "Carla was overwhelmed. I just wanted to help her see that at that moment, her daughter's choice about whether to keep her baby was the least of her worries."

His gaze was warm, measuring. "You helped that young woman. You made a difference for her, her child and her whole family. It's okay to be proud of that."

The baby lay so still, the only recognizable movement coming from the rise and fall of her chest, and even the breathing she did with assistance.

"I just hope Brooke made the right decision." She still couldn't get past her worries over the baby's fragile health.

"She did...because of you."

The baby startled in her sleep and kicked her feet, her hands fisting as she started to cry. Lilly was stronger than she appeared, all right. The infant's show of strength surprised Shannon almost as much as Carla's change of heart regarding her grandchild. But more surprising than either of those things was that the last comment, that last vote of confidence, had come not from Mark, but from Blake.

Chapter Twelve

Mark moved with efficiency in the locker room, buttoning his navy uniform shirt, pinning on his shield and adjusting his weapon. Normally, after a few days off, he would have been itching to get back to work, suffering from withdrawal from his fellow troopers, who were more a family to him than his real family. Today, though, he only wanted to pull his shift without fanfare and get back home. Just over a week and so much had changed.

He didn't bother telling himself this was only about Blake. Not anymore. Poor timing or not, he wanted to be with Shannon. He wanted to be with her and Blake while mother and son navigated their fledgling relationship. Maybe after that, too. As if he hadn't already learned how fleeting life could be from his parents' early deaths, the scare this week involving that young girl and her baby had served as a stark reminder. He didn't want to waste a moment when he could be with her.

Mark managed to avoid any conversations in the locker room, but as soon as he stepped into the squad room, the heat of dozens of gazes covered him. It came as no surprise that Brody Davison was the first to approach him.

"Well, Trooper Shoffner, how was the vacation?"

"Sunny and relaxing."

Brody gave him a measuring look. "Good tan."

"I try."

Close enough to hear the conversation, Angela Vincent stepped over to join them. "From what I hear, it was a working vacation. How's the work at Hope Haven coming? Wait. Hold out your hands." She waited until he extended his hands and then took her time examining them. "You still have all ten fingers."

"Better check his head for lobotomy wounds." Joe Rossetti laughed at his own joke as he strode over to them, proving that his recent promotion to sergeant hadn't made him any less of a class clown. "Did you hear he's pulling parenting duty now? You became a foster parent to a teenager?"

Mark shrugged, smiling. The sergeant had taken a special interest in anything involving parenting lately since his own wife was expecting their first child.

"He had to do *something* to get Mommy's attention," Angela said with a smirk.

"Yeah, did you see that kid's mom?" Brody asked. "Can't say that I blame him for making the big gesture to get *her* attention."

Mark crossed his arms, planted his feet wide and faced all of them, frowning. "No good deed goes unpunished around here. I was just trying to help out a kid who's been pushed around from foster home to foster home."

"So there's nothing between you and Miss Lyndon?" Angela studied him with a stare that was probably effective when she questioned suspects.

"You mean other than a mutual interest in the welfare of a troubled teen?" he asked, instead of answering. He wished he didn't sound so defensive, but there wasn't anything he could do about it. What had begun as a goal to sever ties between his own past and present had melded into the hope for a future, and he wasn't ready to share that secret hope with anyone yet.

"Relax, Shoffner," Trooper Garrett Taylor said as he joined them in the squad room. "Sensitive, aren't we?"

"He does sound a little sensitive," Brody said.

"I think it was a good thing."

Mark turned toward the voice he'd only heard a few times in the squad room. Trooper Celeste Addington, with her business-only attitude, didn't even look up from the PC where she sat working on a report. She seldom joined in on squad-room banter, but Mark appreciated her support this time.

He also appreciated that Lt. Dawson picked that moment to step in front of the group to give announcements at shift change. The sooner he made it to his patrol car and out from under the microscope of a bunch of law enforcement officers, trained to read when suspects were holding back information, the better. Because he was, and they all knew it.

"See you at the Wildwood?" Garrett asked as he collected his radio off the charger and pulled open the heavy metal door leading to the lot where the patrol cars were parked.

"Well…" Mark shrugged into his heavy coat and collected his cover. Several nights a week they met at the Wildwood Diner after their shift, and Mark seldom missed it. "I probably should get home. Blake starts at the new school tomorrow."

"Oh, that's right." Garrett nodded. "You have a kid at home now."

"You said you have a sitter, right?" Angela asked. "And Blake should already be in bed. You could call and say you'll be a little late."

"Wait." Brody stepped in front of him and whirled to face him. "Who did you say was staying with the boy?"

"I didn't." As soon as he said it, he was sorry. The others had been carrying on various conversations as they crossed the parking lot to their cars, but their chatter died at his words. "Shannon…Miss Lyndon is watching him. She needed the chance to get to know Blake. And it wouldn't be right to leave her there longer than necessary when she should be getting back to Hope Haven."

"It's very kind of you not to want to inconvenience her," Angela said, fighting back a smile.

"Well." Brody cleared his throat. "Safe travels out there, everyone."

They all turned away then, and Mark didn't miss the grins they all were trying to hide. Someone chuckled, too, covering it up with a cough. They didn't believe him. Didn't believe that he'd become a foster parent for Blake's sake alone. Didn't buy that he'd volunteered to do work at Hope Haven out of the decency of his heart. Wouldn't accept that there wasn't more to this story, and that this *more* had everything to do with Shannon Lyndon. He couldn't blame them for not believing him because, even from the beginning, he hadn't bought any of his story himself.

Shannon tried to keep her attention on the family sitcom playing on Mark's television that night, but the boy sitting next to her on the sofa kept drawing her focus away from the pithy lines and canned laughter. The funny thing was Blake appeared to be sneaking glances at her just as frequently as she was peeking at him.

That he hadn't immediately locked himself in his room as he'd done the first time she'd stayed with him, combined with his comment of support at the hospital, had given her cause to hope. When he shifted and turned to face her, she straightened in her seat. Would this be it? Would this be the moment when he finally forgave her? Would he tell her that as soon as the courts allowed it and as soon as she could find a place for them other than a home with a dozen—eleven now—pregnant teens, he wanted to live with her?

The longer he waited to say anything, the more anxious she became. Where earlier today it had seemed like a great idea to accept her mother's dinner invitation and include Mark and Blake in it, now she worried it was too soon. Would they think it was a bad idea when she told them about it?

"So what's the deal with you and Mark?"

It was the last thing she expected him to say. Only when Blake grinned at her did she realize that her mouth was hanging open, a landing pad for flies. She clicked her teeth shut.

"Well?" he prompted, still smiling.

She crossed her arms, suddenly cold though she already had a quilt over her lap. If her son had noticed something between her and Mark, then she hadn't done as good a job as she'd thought of keeping her feelings private. Whether or not Mark had any feelings for her, he probably knew exactly how she felt about him.

"I'm not sure what's happening between him and me," she admitted finally. But once she started talking, she didn't seem to be able to stop. "I don't want you to worry, though. No matter what, you are my top priority. So if you don't want Mark and me to see each other, not that we are really seeing each other, but—"

"He's a great guy."

Shannon's eyes widened. "What?"

"He's a great guy. You know that. Even if he is a cop. What other guy would have taken in a delinquent like me? He didn't even have kids of his own."

"I know." She squinted, studying him. "So what you're saying is…?"

Blake shrugged. "That I don't care one way or another."

His comment should have been freeing. She didn't have to forfeit her relationship with her son for a possible connection with the man she just might be in love with. Strangely, though, his words left her feeling empty. Right now her relationship with Blake was still a maybe, and possibilities with Mark were still just that, as well.

For a few minutes, Blake stared at the screen where the comedy played, but he didn't laugh at the punch lines, never even cracking a smile. Finally, he faced her again.

"So what's the story with Chelsea?"

"What do you mean?" she asked cautiously.

"You know. She said she just turned fifteen and that she's from Keego Harbor…."

Somehow Shannon managed not to wince. Even if she'd wanted to, she couldn't tell him details about one of her residents. She hadn't missed that Blake and Chelsea always seemed to end up together at meals during his work at Hope Haven or that Chelsea had saved a few slices of her pumpkin pie with his name written on the plastic wrap. This had *crush* written all over it, and heartbreak etched on top of that. She regretted that she'd introduced Blake to the girls, but if Mark and Blake hadn't spent time at Hope Haven, she might never have gotten to know him at all.

"You know, now might not be the best time for a romance with Chelsea. It's just not—"

"You don't think I'm good enough for her."

He spat the words so fast that her neck snapped back in response. Where a few seconds before he'd been sitting close enough that she could have reached out to touch him if she dared, now he'd backed all the way up to the sofa's edge and crossed his arms over his chest.

"Now, why would you think something like that?"

Blake blinked and then shook his head as if he, too, realized he'd overreacted. "Because I have a record."

"Of course you're good enough for— I mean, you're good enough for any girl you're interested in." She cleared her throat. "But Chelsea—"

"Is this because she's pregnant?"

"Well," she began cautiously. "That is kind of a problem right now."

"You're a hypocrite. You got pregnant yourself, so don't go around thinking you're so much better than she is. She's a great girl. Just because some creep walked out on her doesn't mean—"

Shannon shook her head until her son finally stopped. "You're misunderstanding me. I adore Chelsea. I love all of the girls. I just don't think that right now, while she's expecting a baby, it would be the best time for her to become involved with any young man."

"You're so selfish."

"What?" She felt like a tennis ball being volleyed back and forth, never given the relief of a bounce on the

court in between. Blake was determined to fight with
her no matter what she said.

"Just because you didn't have anyone there with you,
just because my DNA-donor dad took off when you got
pregnant, you don't want anyone to be there for any of
the girls." He jumped up from the couch and looked
down on her. "You don't want Chelsea to have anyone
at all. You just don't get it."

With that, he marched out of the room. From the
sounds of his stomping, he continued up the stairs and
down the hall until a door slam marked his return to his
room. What had just happened? How had they ended up
back here? Tonight might have started out more prom-
ising than that first night when Blake had been left in
her care, but now it was just like before. He was holed
up in his room again, and whether she was physically
upstairs or not, she was still on the outside of his door,
knocking and begging to be let into his life.

He'd come looking for her, and yet he would never
fully accept her. He would never forgive her either, for
something that wasn't totally her fault. How could he
say such hateful things to her? He'd almost sounded
like…her. Not the things she'd ever spoken aloud to her
parents, but those she'd whispered under her breath or
repeated in the privacy of her thoughts. *You just don't
get it*. She'd once said those exact words to her parents
when they'd insisted that she give up her baby. She'd
certainly heard her girls say things like that when referring to their parents.

She'd been sitting cross-legged beneath the quilt, but
now her feet slipped down, and the blanket dropped si-
lently to the floor. The girls had said things like that to
her about their parents, and Blake had said them to her.
His mother. She grinned toward the staircase but didn't

get up to climb it. Her teenage son needed some space tonight, and she would give it to him. She'd wanted to be a mother to Blake, wanted the chance she'd missed out on fifteen years ago, and this was it. For the first time, she'd just experienced real parenting.

"Wake up, Sleeping Beauty."

Shannon startled, an electric hum inside alerting her to Mark's nearness even before her eyes opened. He stood in the doorway across the room, his hands in his pockets. Caught, she sat up from where she'd stretched out on the sofa and tossed off the quilt she'd pulled over herself. She chose to take the words he'd selected to awaken her at face value. It was safer that way.

"Some babysitter you are. Sleeping on the job," he said with a grin.

She frowned as she folded the blanket and threw it over the arm of the sofa. As if it wasn't bad enough that her hair nearly stood on end every time she and Mark passed each other in the hall, now she was having lace-and-baby's-breath dreams about him even when she was asleep.

"Where's Blake, anyway?"

"He's been in his room for hours."

"You sure of that?"

She smiled. They'd had a conversation similar to this one not so long ago.

"The stairs squeak."

"Fair." He glanced over his shoulder at the stairs, and then his head whipped back around. "Wait. You mean he actually took my advice and went to bed early so he'd be fresh for his first day at the new school?"

Her expression must have been telling because his

eyes widened. "You're kidding. He spent the whole night in his room *again?*"

Her cheeks felt hot. "Not the whole night."

He raised a brow, waiting for her to explain.

She blew out a tired breath. "It started out pretty well, but it went downhill fast after I told him this wasn't the best time for Chelsea to become involved with a guy."

"I could have seen that one coming." He crossed the room and took a spot on the other end of the sofa. "Remember, I sat next to them at Thanksgiving dinner."

"You could have given me the heads-up."

"Would it have changed anything?"

She shrugged. "Probably not. I still would have thought that during their pregnancies was a bad time for any of the girls to become involved with new guys. They have too many other things to deal with. And Blake would still have called me a hypocrite."

He held his hands wide, indicating that she'd confirmed his point. "You're not a hypocrite."

"I hope not."

"You're not."

"I felt like a real parent tonight."

"That you are."

At his quietly offered words of support, their gazes connected, and the spacious room suddenly seemed tiny, disturbingly intimate. Mark still sat in the same spot on the sofa, hadn't moved an inch closer, and yet she felt as if he'd just gathered her in a hug. She wanted that very thing more than she could remember wanting anything, except maybe for the chance to know her son. Was it possible that God had intended for Mark and her to be together? That He'd used Blake to bring them together?

She peeked over at him, only to find him watching her, waiting, for what she wasn't certain.

"Are you…uh…ready to put Blake on the big yellow bus for the first time tomorrow?" Did her question sound as ridiculous to him as it had to her?

"Readier than he is, I'm afraid."

She nodded. She had plenty of experience with the challenge of helping the girls keep up with their studies, but for him, this was all new. "He'll do great. You both will. If he's having trouble with algebra, I can help him when I come over in the evenings."

"I'm good at math, too."

"Then we'll both help him," she said with a smile.

"We both are."

She swallowed. Either she was reading messages into everything he said, or he was purposely infusing his words with warmth. She wished with everything inside of her for the second option.

"Uh. Thanks. Well, I'd better get home." She stood up from the couch and crossed to the entry closet where she'd hung her peacoat.

"Ooo-kay," he said in that slow way people had of saying that word when things weren't fine at all.

He thought she was running, but she wasn't. Not really. She was just delaying a little. She wanted a relationship with Mark, but for there to be a real chance for them to build any sort of future together, she needed to tie up the loose ends of her past. Was it time to stop running, hiding, and take a risk? Drawing in a deep breath, she turned to face Mark, who'd stood up from the sofa but hadn't followed her.

"When is your next day off?" she asked.

"Thursday."

"Then Thursday it is."

Instead of continuing to play along, he tilted his head and waited for her to fill in the blanks.

"My parents are back from Guatemala," she explained as she stuffed her hands in her pockets. "They wanted to have dinner with me sometime this week."

"Oh." He nodded as if he understood. "Sure. I can be home with Blake on Thursday night."

She shook her head. "That's not what I meant. I didn't know whether it was too soon, but anyway, I asked them if I could invite you and Blake to join us."

"You're serious? You told them everything?" His eyes had gone wide.

She swallowed. "Well, not everything, but—"

"Enough, right?"

He crossed the room to her in a few long strides. Stopping in front of her, he rested his hands beneath both of her elbows and searched her face. "Were they okay with you bringing Blake?"

"Sure. They were okay with it."

Her thoughts raced. She'd told them she was bringing her friend and his foster son, but that was as far as it had gone. No matter how many times she'd tried, she hadn't been able to find the words to tell them that the boy coming to their house was their own grandson.

Mark must have missed her reticence because his grip tightened slightly, his thumbs caressing her elbows. Even through two layers of cloth, her arms tingled from his gentle touch.

"And what did you tell them about us?"

"Is there an *us?*" she croaked.

"Oh, yeah."

He dipped his head until only a breath of distance separated them, and then he paused, as if waiting for permission. She should have delayed, reflected, as well. They still hadn't discussed what that first kiss had meant, and yet here they were again. But the idea of kissing Mark felt too much like returning home after an endless journey. Too much like the most wonderful story where all the pieces fit perfectly together in the end. Instead of waiting, she lifted herself on her tiptoes and touched her lips to his. Not just receiving his kiss but offering her own.

The strength, the warmth, the kindness that Mark always emitted in waves came together in the sweetness of his kiss. So it surprised her when his arms closed around her, and he pressed his lips firmly against hers in a kiss too fierce to be gentle, brimming with raw emotion. It felt like a promise ripped from the depths of his heart. He released her, but it was with obvious reluctance.

The moment should have been perfect, but she ached with guilt a few minutes later as she waved goodbye and escaped through his front door. With her kiss, she'd told him the truth in her heart. Whether she'd spoken the words aloud or not, she loved him in a way that should be shouted from rooftops or written by planes in the sky. Unfortunately, she'd lied to him, or at least lied by omission, at the same time. And she didn't know what he would do when he realized the truth.

Chapter Thirteen

Had he felt this nervous on his first date? Mark didn't even have to think about the answer to that one. It would be a resounding *no*. Strange…though tonight really wasn't a date, he would still be put to the test of having to meet Shannon's parents.

He pulled his truck to the curb in front of a modest Walled Lake two story and glanced first at Shannon and then in the rearview mirror at Blake. He'd become so accustomed to Blake's fidgeting that he would have been more concerned if the boy was sitting too still. But the way that Shannon wrung her hands in her lap now made him wonder if she was trying to emulate her child.

"Is this your house?"

He reached for her hand, but she startled and pulled it away to open the door.

"Yes, it is," she said as her feet touched the ground. "This is where I spent my first eighteen years."

Except for a short time when her parents had sent her away, he wanted to add, but didn't. He had to meet the people who'd made that decision tonight, and if he planned to be civil to her parents, he couldn't keep reminding himself about how they'd treated her.

"Are we going in or what?" Blake asked as he climbed down to the running board.

Shannon shot a look at the front of the house as if she expected someone to peek out from behind the curtains over the picture window. Mark couldn't blame her for being nervous. No matter how proud he was of her for moving past her resentment to give Blake the chance for a relationship with his grandparents, being there to-night was probably scraping against old scars.

Mark had just climbed down from the truck and had rounded the bed when the glass front door swung wide and a silver-headed couple stepped out onto the porch, the woman drawing a long sweater closer over her shoulders. Even from a distance, Mark could see that Shannon looked a little like her father, but she more strongly resembled her mother, with her pale skin, fine features and long hair that might once have been deep brown. As they drew closer, another pair of familiar hazel eyes peered out at him from behind her mother's gold-framed glasses.

"Hi, Mom. Hi, Dad." Shannon climbed the steps and hugged each of them before indicating the two guys behind her. "I'd like you to meet Mark Shoffner and Blake Wilson."

"Mark, Blake, please meet my parents, Roger and Marilyn Lyndon."

"It's a pleasure to meet you," Roger said, speaking for the both of them. "Welcome to our home."

Mark didn't know what he'd expected. That they would have grabbed the boy and sandwiched him be-tween them in a reunion hug? Or that they would have offered tearful apologies? But he hadn't expected them to greet Blake like a stranger. Even if that was exactly what he was.

Suddenly, Marilyn gestured toward the house. "Well, come on inside before you all catch your death."

Now, the inside of the Lyndon home, Mark might have expected. Formal. Immaculate. Everything in its place. Shannon had once been a piece out of place in their perfect world, and she'd been sent away so they could pretend that nothing had changed when everything had.

"It smells great in here," Blake remarked, speaking for the first time since his grandparents had appeared. If he believed their introduction was strange, he didn't mention it.

"I trust your drive wasn't too bad." Marilyn closed the door behind them and tightened her sweater again, securing it with its belt. "The traffic is always so congested on that interstate."

Mark shrugged. "It was fine. Besides, I'm pretty used to driving on I-96. Shannon told you I'm a Michigan State trooper, didn't she?"

Her eyes widened, but then she pushed aside his question with a brush of her hand. "Uh, I'm sure she did. It just slipped my mind."

Somehow Mark doubted that anything had slipped. More likely Shannon hadn't told her what he did for a living. Had she said anything at all about him other than that he was coming for dinner? Did she not want her parents to know that she and he were involved— well, that they were on the verge of being involved? Was Shannon worried her parents wouldn't accept him because he was divorced?

"I hope you two like roast beef because my wife has made enough for an army. And for dessert, we have raspberry cheesecake." Roger directed them toward the dining room, where the table was beautifully set with a floral centerpiece holding court among several platters of food. "We don't often have dinner guests."

Mark guessed that visits from their grandson were rarer still, but he managed not to say so. "It looks as if you're old pros at it. This is amazing."

Marilyn glowed under his praise. "Let me get the main dish."

She disappeared into the kitchen and returned with a huge platter of roast beef and roasted potatoes. She took her seat and invited the others to sit, as well.

Roger stood to say grace. "Thank you, Father, for bringing us together today. Please bless this food and teach us to do Your will. Amen."

"Amen," Mark repeated. It wasn't the prayer that he would have given on a momentous day like today, but maybe Shannon's father wasn't into making big statements.

"So, Blake," Roger began as he started passing platters and filling his plate. "How are you enjoying your new school?"

"Uh, it's fine," Blake managed.

Mark couldn't help but chuckle. The boy was on his best behavior if he was calling school "fine." He was trying to make a good impression on his grandparents.

Roger turned to Mark. "I heard you say you work for the state police. How long have you been keeping our community safe?"

"Well, Southeast Michigan specifically, only a few months, but I've been with the state police eight years."

Marilyn turned to her daughter. "And I trust that the girls at Hope Haven are doing well?"

Shannon nodded but, strangely, didn't mention Brooke or the dramatic events last week.

The conversation seemed to be going well, even if the

Lyndons weren't asking what Mark believed were the right questions. They talked about their mission trip to Guatemala, for which they seemed to have a true calling rather than just an excuse to miss the Hope Haven Thanksgiving celebration.

Roger took a bite of his roast beef and then wiped his mouth on a napkin. "Shannon, you never told us how you became acquainted with Mark and his foster son."

Foster son? Immediately, all the fragmented pieces fell into place, and fury and hurt rose together inside him, both competing to dominate his emotions. Blake appeared confused, having yet to realize that his mother had betrayed him. Mark's hands gripped the edge of the table, but for some reason, he couldn't speak up. It was like watching two cars racing toward each other on an icy road. Tragedy was inevitable, and he could only sit there and stare.

"No, Dad, I didn't." She indicated Blake with a wide sweep of her hand. "But I thought you might recognize Blake because he's my son."

"What?" Roger asked, though from his stark expression, it was clear that he'd heard her.

"Yes, Grandma and Grandpa, I'd like you to meet your only grandson."

Marilyn let out a sharp cry and covered her face with her hands.

"Almost two weeks ago Blake showed up on my doorstep, hungry, in trouble with the law and the victim of a state system that the three of us sentenced him to."

Marilyn looked up and started shaking her head. "No. He was *adopted* by good parents. They went to church."

"Apparently, they also cared more about their drug habit than they did my son," Shannon told them.

Like his wife, Roger shook his head. "We wanted to do the right thing."

"The right thing for whom, Dad? For Blake? For me? Or just for you and Mom, so you didn't have to be humiliated by your imperfect daughter?"

"We didn't know." He squeezed his eyes shut, and then he turned to Blake. "We're sorry, son. So sorry."

The scene was eerily familiar. Different setting. Different cast of characters. But the same blame was being tossed around like a weapon with intent to injure. Succeeding. He'd thought tonight was a statement about a family he and Shannon might build together with Blake. Instead, she'd made them complicit in her ruse.

Without ever hearing her parents' side in the story regarding Blake's adoption, he'd judged them. He always listened to both sides in an investigation before coming to any conclusions, but he'd allowed his feelings for Shannon to color his thoughts. And the one who would be hurt most by his mistake was Blake.

The boy didn't even move, his hands still in a way they never were. His eyes were glazed, his skin pallid.

"We're out of here." Mark leaped up from the table so quickly that the formal dining chair flipped backward, landing with a bang on the hardwood floor. He righted it and then stepped over to take Blake's arm. "Let's go."

He prepared himself for a hit in case the boy struck out at him, but Blake only stood and allowed Mark to lead him from the room.

Shannon stood up, as well. "Mark, what are you doing?"

"We've already performed our roles in the trick you wanted to play on your parents. We're done. We're going home now."

Roger crossed to his wife and helped her up from the chair.

"What have we done?" She sobbed into his arms.

Shannon stared at the chaos erupting all around her, a mess so awful that it must have been caused by someone else. What had she been thinking? She wanted to believe that the situation simply hadn't turned out the way she'd planned, but it was clear that she hadn't had a plan at all, other than to shock her parents the way she'd thought they deserved to be shocked.

But had they deserved that? No matter what mistakes they'd made—any of them had made—it had been unfair to shake them up by announcing Blake's identity that way. Her son hadn't deserved to be thrown in his grandparents' faces like a bucket of slime either, any more than Mark had deserved to be blindsided by her plan. How could she have done something like that to her own son *and* the man she loved?

Her father led her mother from the room, but he paused at the door. "It might be best if you went with them."

"Sorry, Dad. Mom."

"Not now."

Mark and Blake were already in the truck, and Mark had started the engine by the time that Shannon reached them. She stood outside the door and waited. He looked straight ahead, his hands squeezing the steering wheel. Finally, he reached for the button and lowered the window.

"Get in."

If her car hadn't already been parked at his house, he probably would have driven off and left her there. With the truck already in gear, he jammed the gas pedal as soon as she'd closed the door and clicked her seat belt. The silence was so intense on the return ride to Brighton that Shannon could hear her heart thrumming in her ears. Blake remained so still that she would have given anything to feel him tapping his foot against the back of her seat. She'd brought this on herself, and she would have to live with the consequences.

"Blake, could you go ahead inside?" Mark asked as soon as he parked the truck outside of his house.

"No problem."

After Mark opened the door and pulled forward the seat to let him out, Blake climbed down and jogged toward the house. Shannon thought she saw him looking back once, but that might have been wishful thinking. Her son would probably never forgive her now, and she had no one to blame but herself.

As soon as Blake was gone, Mark climbed back into the truck, closing the door, but instead of allowing the cab to return to darkness, he flipped on the dome light.

"I can't believe you did that. Not just to me, either. But to your parents and, especially, to Blake. Did you even think—"

"No. I didn't." She shook her head. "I'm so sorry. I was going to tell them the truth before we went, but when I tried, all I could bring myself to tell them was that I was inviting my friend and his foster son."

Mark gripped the steering wheel so hard his knuckles flashed white. "Bring yourself to tell them? You planned that whole thing so you could surprise them with your fourteen-year-old baby boy."

"That wasn't it. I just couldn't—"

But he shook his head to interrupt her. "You just wanted to hurt them as much as you could to repay them for their mistakes fifteen years ago. Well, you succeeded. Did it make you feel stronger to watch your mother cry?"

"No." Her own eyes flooded with tears. It hadn't felt good or justified. "Please. I'm so sorry. I don't know what I was thinking."

"You should tell *them* that. Whatever your mom and dad did, they didn't deserve that. You wanted to prove something to them, and you didn't think twice about using your son and me to do it. Didn't we mean any—"

He cut himself off, squeezing his eyes shut, his jaw flexing as he gritted his teeth.

Shannon reached out to touch his arm. "I was wrong. I couldn't have been more wrong. Please, Mark, you've got to forgive me."

"Got to?"

He stared down at her fingers on his arm until she pulled them away. The engine hadn't been turned off long enough for the truck cab to be chilly, and yet she shivered. Hopelessness settled deep inside her.

"How can you expect me, Blake or your parents to forgive you when you never forgive anyone? I know it says somewhere in the Bible that you must forgive to be forgiven. When will you give up this grudge you've been holding against your parents? When will you realize that there was plenty of guilt to go around in that whole situation?"

Her breath caught, and she backed away from him, pressing her shoulder blades into the truck door. "Who are you to criticize my feelings about my parents? You, the guy who's still chasing after *his* parents' approval, even after they've been gone."

"We're not talking about me. We're talking about you and the cruel joke you played on everyone. Anyway, you don't know anything about my parents. Or me."

"Don't I?" She stared at him, refusing to back down just because he'd tried to turn the conversation back to her. "I know that you're allowing your desperate search for redemption to keep you from living your life. You talk about forgiveness, and yet you don't believe that you've already received it. Deep in your heart, you know your parents forgave you for the stuff that happened when you were a kid. God forgave you the minute you asked. Even your friend, Chris, forgave you, even though his wheelchair was a permanent reminder of the accident."

She needed to stop talking, but the momentum was too strong, carrying her like a locomotive traveling at top speed. She tried to put on the brakes, but the wheels continued turning and the words kept spilling.

"You're the only one who refuses to forgive you," she told him. "The only one with something to prove. And you've already allowed this mission of yours to ruin one marriage through lack of effort. If you're not careful, you'll allow this pointless quest to prove you're not that guy anymore to push away everyone who ever loves you."

Like me. She swallowed. Somehow she'd managed not to say it, but if he were listening, he could have heard the words that she'd implied. From what she could tell, he hadn't been. At least not closely enough to have really heard her.

In the same way she had, Mark had backed up to the truck door and sat with his arms crossed, staring her down in a face-off of anger and blame. In the silence that filled the cab, it appeared as if he wouldn't answer her at all, but then he spoke again in a tight voice.

"You don't know anything about what destroyed my marriage. Or anything about marriage at all. You were burned one time when you were a kid, and you never took a risk on a relationship again. Too afraid of getting hurt. You don't know what it's like to commit your life to someone and then have her cheat and blame you for it."

His words struck her like repeated blows to the heart. She braced herself, hoping to deflect the pain, but it seeped in through every pore. He was right; she didn't know what it was like to be betrayed that way, although the betrayal she'd experienced had been painful enough. He was right about the other things, too, including that she'd been afraid to ever risk her heart again.

But on one matter, Mark was dead wrong. She had taken a risk. Despite impossible timing. Despite all of the warnings she'd given herself. Despite everything. She'd taken that risk for him. She'd allowed him to chisel away at the wall she'd built to shield her heart and then granted him admission, trusting him not to hurt her. She should have known better.

"But you do know about blaming other people," he said.

Shannon had been staring at her hands, but at his words, she looked up at him again. "I don't know what you're talking about."

"You blame everyone else for your mistakes. You never take responsibility for your part in the situations."

"That's rich coming from you," she spat. "Have you looked in the mirror and then back at your divorce decree? It's easy for you to blame your ex-wife for her indiscretions, but are you blameless in the collapse of your marriage? She said you were married to the job. Have you ever thought that while you were out chasing commendations for a decorated police career that she was home alone waiting for you to realize that she mattered?"

Mark shifted, sitting taller in the seat. "If you haven't seen yourself in that mirror, I would look again. You have nobody to blame but yourself for becoming involved with a creep when you knew he was one. And you're the one who got pregnant, though obviously you couldn't get there alone. Your folks might have made big mistakes dealing with their pregnant daughter, but the mess was yours."

Shannon gritted her teeth and squeezed her eyes shut, watching multicolored spots dance inside her eyelids, before she could finally look at him again. "I suppose it was also my fault that Blake's adoptive parents had their rights terminated and he ended up bouncing around the system for years?"

He shook his head. "I never said that. But I am saying that you need to stop blaming everyone else for the things that *were* your responsibility. Blake deserves better than that from his mother."

"You mean from his *birth* mother, don't you?" She slammed her hand on the dash so hard her palm ached, but she didn't care. "You've judged me from the minute you set eyes on me. You've never thought I deserved the chance to build a relationship with my son."

"Are you kidding? I'm the one who's made it *possible* for you to build something with him by giving him a place to live."

"You've stood in the way every chance you've had, too. Well, thanks for stepping up to be his foster parent, but you won't have to deal with him, or me, much longer. As soon as the court grants me custody, neither of us will ever bother you again."

With that she threw the door open, climbing down

the step. But Mark's words followed her out into the cold before she could close the door.

"Why do you think you should be given custody of Blake when you voluntarily gave him away?"

Chapter Fourteen

Mark felt as if he'd parked his truck on his chest instead of on the driveway by the time that he pushed his front door open and stepped inside. Why he'd had to take that final unacceptable jab, he didn't know, but if the whole argument had gone too far, the last had made the rest seem like a friendly disagreement. The worst part was he'd wanted to hurt her, just like her actions and words tonight had cut him more deeply than a switchblade ever could. And from the way she'd slammed the truck door and had run to her car, he'd done a bang-up job of it.

Shannon deserved it. She'd used him like a pawn in a silly game of revenge where everyone got hurt. He should have known better than to put so much stock in the meeting with her parents. The night was supposed to be about Blake, anyway—not him. Yet he'd allowed himself to believe that she was making a statement about the future she wanted with him, as well. Worse than angry and betrayed, he felt duped.

Yes, she'd deserved the things he'd said, but that didn't make him feel any less like a heel. He wanted to take it all back, but it was too late. The words had been destructive. And hers had been dead wrong. Whatever hope they'd had for a relationship was gone, as well. No one could come back from the things she'd done, the things they'd said. Like a roller-coaster ride, they'd squeezed a whole relationship into a single night: the anticipation of the first hill, the heights and the dips of the ride and the screeching halt of the end.

The darkness in the living room came as a relief. Blake was a smart boy. He'd probably jumped into bed and covered his head with a pillow. Who could blame him? He might eventually want to talk about the scene at his grandparents' house, but Mark planned to give him a free pass tonight. He wanted one of those himself.

He'd made it to the center of the living room, just behind the sofa, when the table lamp in the corner flipped on with a click. Mark blinked at the sudden intrusion of light. Blake sat in the old plaid recliner, his sock-clad feet elevated, crossed at the ankles.

"You blew it, didn't you?"

Mark rested against the back of the sofa and tilted his head to the side. "What are you talking about?"

Blake lifted a brow. "Oh, I don't know. Maybe that whole knock-down-drag-out argument you just had under the truck's dome light with Miss Shannon."

He indicated the window through which he'd had a perfect view of the two of them inside the truck.

"You watched the whole time?"

"There wasn't anything good on TV."

But the leftover crusts of a peanut-butter sandwich and the empty glass of milk on the table showed that he'd found something to entertain himself with at least part of the time.

"Did you fight about me?" Blake asked quietly.

"Among other things."

"Did you win?"

Mark could only shake his head.

"Did she?"

Tilting his head to the side, Mark lifted a brow. The boy understood far more than he'd realized.

"No, I don't think anyone won tonight."

But *he'd* definitely lost. Then as Shannon's words from earlier filtered through his thoughts, it became clear that he wasn't the only one. *Everyone who ever loves you.* She'd all but admitted that she loved him, and no matter how much he'd refused to admit it, he loved her, too. As if that could matter now. The sudden pain in his chest was visceral, as if he was being ripped apart on the inside while on the outside he appeared untouched. Sure, he loved her, but he couldn't be with someone as unbending and unforgiving as she was. He couldn't.

Blake was still watching him when he looked up again, and the kid grinned at him though tonight hadn't given any of them a reason to smile.

"I don't get something," Mark said. "You of all people have every right to be furious with Shannon for throwing you in her parents' faces. But you aren't, are you?"

"Why should I be? She just did what she thought she needed to do to make a statement."

"But she *used* you to do it."

"I guess so."

The boy's lack of indignation only bothered him more. "But that was the way you had to meet your grandparents."

"I always like to make a great first impression. Remember the way I met my… Miss Shannon?"

Mark couldn't believe his ears. After everything

Shannon had done to him tonight, Blake was still tempted to call her his mom.

"Was it strange meeting the people who'd insisted that your mother give you away?"

"Sure, it was strange. I tried to remember that back then they were parents, just trying to do what they thought was best for their kid, who'd made a big mistake."

"You were *not* a mistake."

Mark's own words surprised him, coming out louder and with more intensity than he'd planned.

Blake chuckled as he flicked off the lamp. "Good to know, Trooper Shoffner. Now I have to go to bed. Tomorrow's a school day."

"Blake," he called after him until the boy stopped. "You don't really blame your mom for the things that happened to you after she placed you for adoption either, do you?"

"Nah. She couldn't have known."

"Have you ever thought about telling her that? I'm sure she'd like to know."

"Yeah. I could."

Mark continued to watch Blake's figure in shadow as the boy went up the stairs. It didn't make any sense. The same angry boy who'd come to the area to pummel with blame the adults who'd wronged him had forgiven them all so easily. Why couldn't he do that? He was the Christian, so how was it that a troubled kid who hadn't made his peace with God yet was teaching him about forgiveness?

Mark rounded the sofa and slumped into the cushions in the dark. The boy becoming *his* teacher was ironic, but it was just as ironic that he'd convinced himself he couldn't be with someone as unforgiving as Shannon was. And yet he was just like her.

He shoved his hands back through his hair, replaying their hateful accusations. Her words had been biting, but they were also true. It was so easy for him to blame Kim for the failure of their marriage without taking any responsibility for his role in it. How could he have had time to put the necessary work into a marriage when he was so busy chasing the impossible approval of his parents, who weren't even there to give it? Had she been lonely all those nights while he'd worked late? Sure, his ex-wife would never be blameless in the situation, but he'd helped to build the trap that had ensnared her. For the first time, he was ready to take responsibility for his role and to finally forgive her.

Was he also ready to forgive Shannon? If Blake could do it, so could he. That was what people who loved each other did. And he did love her. Until this moment he hadn't realized how much. The woman he'd held in his arms just twice was the only woman he could ever imagine in that space for the rest of his life. So he hated the sinking feeling that his love wouldn't be enough to restore this broken picture. He hated the awful things he'd said, particularly the one about her giving up her child. How could he have been so cruel as to attack her where she was most vulnerable? Things once said couldn't be unsaid, and the one he'd spoken had been the worst of all.

For several seconds, he cradled his head in his hands, wishing there were something he could do. And then he realized that there was. He wasn't sure if he and Shannon could ever get past what had happened tonight, but there were still some things he could do for the woman he loved. He could be there for Blake, ensuring that the boy remained close by until he could finally build a home with his mother. He had to make sure that the boy wasn't moved to a more permanent foster home in the meantime. That meant he had to complete his certification.

Checking the time on his cell phone, he wondered if it would be too late to call tonight. But he couldn't wait until office hours, and someone had made the mistake of giving him her personal cell number, so he dialed it. When a sleepy Miss Lafferty picked up on the third ring, he smiled. Yes, he could do this one thing for Shannon and Blake. He would always want more than this, but he would have to satisfy himself with the knowledge that he'd done the right thing at least once.

"What's wrong, Miss Shannon?"

At the sound of Kelly's voice, Shannon blinked, and she squeezed harder on the door frame that she was using to hold herself up. The rest of the world beyond its firm wood surety—the walls, the desks, the windows— were in a constant state of sway. She'd lost the man she loved last night through her own stupidity, and now she'd lost her son as well, through a situation that was beyond her control.

"Are you okay?" Chelsea rushed over to her at what in advanced pregnancy passed for top speed and tucked a hand under her elbow. "I know you had a phone call. Did you get bad news?"

"Here, let me help."

Holly took the other elbow, and they led her to one of the computer chairs the other girls had set out for her. Absently, Shannon noticed it was the same chair where Holly had been sitting two weeks before when the girl had first felt her baby move. Where Shannon had experienced those last few minutes while her secret was still hers alone and while the meeting she'd planned with Blake was still somewhere in the far-off future, still pristine in its possibilities. Even knowing everything she knew now, even knowing this horrible call would come, she wouldn't have changed a thing about that day.

"Is it Blake?" Tonya asked, pushing up her glasses on her nose. "Or is it Mark…er, Trooper Shoffner?"

Shannon shook her head as she tried to sit up in the seat, her head spinning as if she'd stood too quickly. "It's nothing. They're fine. Everyone's fine. Really."

Kelly kneeled in front of her and looked into her eyes. "*You* don't look fine."

Shannon forced her best smile, blinking hard to push back the tears that would give her away. "Well, I am."

She scanned the concerned faces around her. The last thing she needed was to send the girls into a tizzy and set off a chorus of Braxton-Hicks contractions in those girls nearing full term.

"Now, isn't this a little backward, girls? I'm supposed to be taking care of you."

"And you do a great job of it," Sam told her. "Most of the time. But who takes care of you?"

Who, indeed? She used to think she didn't need anyone. That she was safer, happier even, relying only on herself. Now she'd had a taste of what it was like to have arms ready to catch her when she lost her footing, and she couldn't imagine returning to that solitary existence. Still, that was what she had to do.

Tonya squeezed in front of the others and held out a small stack of pink message forms with While You Were Out emblazoned across the top. "A couple of calls came in while you were on your cell phone in the other room."

Reaching for them, Shannon was relieved that she managed to grasp the papers without sending them flying all over the floor. Two were from her parents, but she wasn't ready to talk to them yet. She owed them an apology, and she would need to prepare herself for that. Two more were from different troopers at the Michigan State Police Brighton Post, each requesting times for bringing out groups of volunteers for service projects. The fifth was from Mark. Unlike the first four, with their dutiful recordings of times, dates and return numbers, the fifth had only *Trooper Shoffner* listed on the name line and *Call ASAP* on the message line.

It didn't matter that she was still reeling from last night's events or that his parting crack had foreshadowed the news she received this morning. She still had to return his call. After the things they'd both said last night, he never would have called if it weren't important.

"I'd better take this in my office."

She stood, relieved that her legs were somewhat sturdy beneath her. As she started from the room, she selected Mark's name from the list of contacts on her cell and pushed Send. He answered on the second ring.

"Shannon? What is it? Is everything all right?"

She glanced back over her shoulder toward the girls, but all of them had picked this particular moment to focus on their computer terminals. The gesture was sweet, even if it was ill timed. One of them had recognized that she'd needed someone and, guessing that Mark was the right person, had ensured she would have the chance to speak to him. Two days ago they would have chosen right.

"I'm okay," she said on a sigh. "I got a message that you'd called, but it must have been a mistake."

It didn't feel like a mistake, though, talking to him again, hearing the quiet strength in his voice. She should have had more pride. He'd used that voice to say the most hateful things to her last night, things intended to hurt her as much as she must have hurt him. But she longed to have him next to her now, that voice near her ear, telling her that everything would be all right.

"Well." An awkward pause filled the phone line before he finally spoke again. "It's…uh…good that you called. I…um…was getting ready to call you."

"You were?" A few hours ago, she would have given anything to hear those words, even like this when he sounded uncomfortable speaking to her. In her dream, he would have said that last night was a horrible mistake, and they could begin again, pretending it never happened. And it would have made a difference. Now it couldn't.

"I have news about Blake."

"I've already heard."

"She called you?"

Shannon blinked. "She?" They both knew her family law attorney was male.

"Miss Lafferty."

"No. Um…I heard from my attorney."

"Wait. Does this mean you received the DNA results?"

"He started out the conversation, 'Do you want the good news or the bad first?'"

"Oh."

Mark had begun a conversation with Blake that same way right after he'd first arrested him, on a day when the good news offered hope and possibilities. From his silence, he must have understood that this time wouldn't be like the one before.

After what seemed like a lifetime in ticking seconds, Mark cleared his throat and spoke up again.

"You don't mean that Blake's not really your—"

"My son?" She hadn't realized that he might jump to that conclusion. Since she'd never questioned it, she was surprised that after everything he could have any doubt. "Oh, he's my son, all right. The test results said that I was 'not excluded from maternity,' and there was a 99.92 percent probability that I was his biological mother."

"That sounds like the good news."

"That part was good."

"Are you going to tell me the bad news?"

Tears escaped from the corners of her eyes before she could open her mouth again. "He said…that I shouldn't get my hopes up…about receiving custody of Blake."

"But that's not new news," he said, seeming to forget his earlier discomfort. "He told you it was going to be a challenge from the beginning. Why would he tell you that now? Was he just trying to upset you?"

"Remember how I told you that as a birth parent who signed a voluntary release of parental rights, I am not one of the parties who can legally request a court modification of a permanent custody order?"

She waited for his affirmative sound before continuing. "Although Miss Lafferty recommended to the Department of Human Services that they support my request, her superiors have chosen…not to file…on my behalf."

Somehow she managed to choke out those last words that felt like nails being pounded into a door that would lock Blake away from her forever. She could call to him through the wood, like she'd done that first night at Mark's house, and could strain to hear him calling back for her, but she had no power to open the door.

"I'm sorry, Shannon. Miss Lafferty didn't tell me."

Using the sleeve of her long-sleeved T-shirt, she brushed aside her tears. They were impotent tears anyway, as incapable of making a difference as she was in providing a home for her own son.

"Wait. Didn't you say you had news, too?"

"It doesn't matter now," he said in a soft voice.

For some reason, hearing Mark sound as defeated as she did crushed her heart even more. Hopelessness enclosed her in its grasp, attempting to swallow her whole. But there were words she still needed to say, even if they wouldn't make any difference now.

"I'm sorry, Mark. For all of those things I said last night."

"I know. I'm sorry, too."

"I'll still be over when Blake gets out of school this afternoon," she told him.

"You're sure?"

"Absolutely."

There were precious few things she was sure of right now, but this was one of them. No matter how painful it was to be in Mark's home and know that she was responsible for destroying what could have been between them, she was determined to keep her commitment to stay with Blake during Mark's work shifts. Her son had to know that his mother wanted him—desperately— and always had.

Even if the courts prevented her from providing a home for him in the way she'd hoped, she never wanted him to doubt, even for a minute, that he was loved. She would spend as much time as she possibly could with him until he was placed again and would continue to visit, if she was allowed to, even after that. Then on his eighteenth birthday, when he was finally free of the state's control, she would invite him to live with her.

Brushing away the last of her tears, Shannon pulled a compact out of her drawer and removed the smudges of her eye makeup with her thumb. She could do this. She would be the best mother she could be to Blake, even if it had to be from a distance. She didn't look forward to delivering the news to him this afternoon, but she would do it as gently as possible.

A knock at the door reminded her that there were others who needed answers from her today. Her girls. She'd once kept the secret of her child from them, but they would be witnesses now as she faced this newest challenge. She hoped she would do it with grace and that they would be proud of her.

"Come in," she called out.

She expected at least six of the girls to spill through the door, their ears red from having pressed them to the wood, but Chelsea was alone as she stepped inside.

"Miss Shannon, can I talk to you for a minute?"

"Sure. Come in and sit." She gestured toward the chair where all of the girls had sat at one time or another to talk during some of the rougher times in their pregnancies.

Shannon sat straighter in her seat. She hadn't had a conversation with the young lady yet regarding Blake, but she prepared her words carefully now. Somehow she needed to convince Chelsea that now wasn't a good time for her to become involved with a boy without leaving the impression that she thought her son was too good for her. She smiled as the conversation she'd had with

Blake came to mind. Hopefully, this one would go more smoothly than the other had.

"I know there's something going on with you today," Chelsea said, gripping her hands together in her lap, "and I'm sorry to add one more thing."

"Whatever it is, we'll work it out together." She cleared her throat. "Now, if this is about Blake..."

"Blake?" She drew her brows together. "What about him?"

"I don't know. I thought you and—"

"Oh. No. We're just friends."

Shannon nodded, though she wondered if her son was aware of how the girl had defined their relationship.

Chelsea patted her stomach and then gripped her hands on top of it. "Besides, I'm taking some time off from guys. I've got more important things on my mind right now."

Again, Shannon nodded. "That's a good idea. Now, you said you had one more thing that we needed to deal with. What is it?"

Chelsea stared at her hands. "I need you to help me go through all the paperwork." She stopped and took a shaky breath. "I've decided to place my baby for adoption. I want to sign the papers today."

Chapter Fifteen

Shannon's eyes burned, and she blinked back tears for the twentieth time since arriving at Mark's house two hours before. And for the twentieth time, Blake pretended not to notice, as he sat at the dining room table, solving again for x and y.

The afternoon had been harder than she'd expected, from pulling into the driveway to passing Mark in the kitchen to watching him back out his truck and drive away. She wanted to believe she could do this, for Blake's sake. But seeing Mark face-to-face was different than speaking to him on the phone, where she'd been able to apologize without having to see in his distant expression how much she'd hurt him. How could she bear being so close to him every day while knowing that they couldn't be together now?

"I still don't know why I need to do my homework on Friday night," Blake groused. "Algebra would still be here Sunday night."

"And you'd still be complaining about having to do it then, though you would have had two extra days since your teacher presented the lesson in class."

"Sounds fishy to me." He frowned and then popped

a cracker with cheese into his mouth. Already, he'd cleared off the plate of grapes and apple slices, and he was mowing down the second plate with cheese and crackers between math problems.

"Oh, I have an agenda, all right. I want you to pass algebra."

He finished the last problem on his homework and shoved the lined paper her way. "Done."

She checked over the answers and grinned at him. "Good job. Now history."

"Ever heard that you're a slave driver?"

"Once or twice."

But he pulled the second textbook out of his backpack and opened it to the pages noted in his planner. "You know," he began too casually, "I called and texted Chelsea a couple of times today, and I didn't hear anything back from her. Did you take her phone away?"

"Of course not. Like always, she couldn't use it during schooltime, meals or chores, but she would have had it during her free time."

"I don't get it, then. She usually texts back." He shrugged as if it didn't matter.

"Blake, there's something you need to know. Today was a tough day for Chelsea. She went before a judge and signed her voluntary release of parental rights."

"And you *let* her?"

She'd expected Blake to strike out; Chelsea's decision hit too close to home for him. But she hadn't prepared herself for the sudden tears in his eyes, the ones he was covering by pretending he had something in his eye.

"It wasn't about *letting* her. It was her choice. I only ensured she had the chance to make it."

He had lifted his arms now to shield his face and was crying into his sleeve. "She'd said she was thinking about doing it, but I told her she didn't have to. I would be there for her, even if her parents weren't. Even if the creep wasn't. But she did it, anyway."

"She made her choice, Blake. And it's a beautiful choice. An amazing gift. She'll help a childless couple to become parents, and she'll know that her child is placed in a loving home. She's working with a private adoption agency on an open adoption, so she can receive updates on her baby as he or she grows up."

Shannon braced herself, expecting Blake to throw the details of his own adoption back at her again, but he only nodded, finally lowering his arm. The sleeve of his blue flannel shirt was wet from his tears.

"You make it sound like such a good thing."

"It can be." She cleared her throat. "You know, the thing that happened in your adoption? Happened to us? It was awful, but it was also incredibly rare."

He surprised her by chuckling. "I get that. We were special."

Shannon made a scoffing sound. "In that case, I would have preferred to be ordinary."

Blake stared out the dining room window. "I told Chelsea I would be there for her if she kept the baby. I had this fantasy that I would swoop in and be Chelsea's rescuer. Maybe even some kind of dad to her baby. Pretty stupid, wasn't it?"

"It wasn't stupid."

Without thinking, Shannon leaned over and did the thing she'd been dying to do for two weeks. She gathered Blake into her arms and kissed his temple. She wasn't sure she would be able to bear the rejection if he pulled away from her, but she did it, anyway. For her son. To her surprise, Blake tucked his head under her chin and held on tight.

Shannon brushed her fingers through his soft hair, comforting the boy in a way she'd never had the chance to console the baby. And he allowed her to do it.

"You're going to be a wonderful dad someday. You're already a good friend. I'm sure that Chelsea appreciated your offer of help. She'll still need support from friends like you as she makes good on her promise to place her child. It won't be easy, even if she knows it's the right thing."

Now Blake did pull back from her and searched her face with questioning eyes. "How can she know it's the right thing?"

"I know it's hard, especially for you, but try to understand where she's coming from. She doesn't feel as if she's ready to be a parent when she's still a kid herself."

"So were you," he said in a soft voice.

Shannon's breath caught. Was Blake finally ready to forgive her for the things that had happened to him? Was he ready to allow her to be a mother to him?

"I want you to know how sorry I am about using you and Mark to shock my parents."

"You've already apologized for it…four times now."

"Still, I really am sorry. I was wrong."

"You've got to give yourself a break once in a while, Miss Shannon," he said with a chuckle. "Anyway, I can understand the behavior of an angry teenager."

"That would make a lot more sense if I was still fifteen instead of thirty."

"Maybe you finally have it out of your system now."

Shannon blew out a breath. "Let's sure hope so. I would say it's about time."

"Don't you think it's also about time for you to forgive *your* parents?"

"Does this mean you've decided to forgive me?"

He brushed his hand across the open page of his history textbook as if to wipe away the past. "Nothing to forgive. Never was. You thought you were doing the best thing for me."

A knot formed in Shannon's throat. This was the moment she'd waited for, prayed for. But Blake had given her more than the forgiveness she'd craved. He'd offered some mature advice, as well. Mark had said it, too, and both of them were right. If she was ever going to be able to move forward with her life, she needed to finally forgive her parents.

"Are you in love with Mark?"

She jerked her head to look at him. Blake only watched her steadily, appearing to wait for her to confirm the answer he already knew.

"Yes...I am." The words sounded like they were ripped from her throat. It felt as if they were. What good did it do to admit it now, when it was too late?

"What are you going to do about it?"

"What do you mean? You know what I did. You were there. I hurt him. I destroyed any possibility for Mark and me to be together."

"You probably thought the same thing about you and me."

Shannon swallowed. "There's something I have to tell you." She took a deep breath and continued. "Although the test came back confirming that you're my son, it's looking less likely that I'm going to be given custody of you."

He listened while she gave him all the details, his expression carefully blank.

"Did anyone ever question whether I was your son?"

"I didn't."

He shook his head. "Me, neither."

"But it had to be documented so that I could—" She stopped herself, squeezing her eyes shut and pressing her lips together before she tried again. "Anyway, you understand what I'm saying, right? As of now, I won't even be allowed to petition the court to have you come live with me. Soon you'll be placed in a permanent foster home, and I'm not even sure whether I'll be given the chance to visit you."

"That won't make you any less my mother."

Shannon swallowed, heat building behind her eyes. "No, it won't. You'll always be my son, no matter where you're staying, and when you're eighteen, you will be welcome to come and live with me."

"You won't expect me to move into your room at Hope Haven, will you?"

She smiled at his attempt to brighten the situation. "No. I can probably get a place that's bigger than ten-by-ten by that time."

For a few minutes, neither said more. Shannon stood and leaned over the table to pick up Blake's plate and milk glass, but as she straightened again, Blake reached for her arm. "Promise me that you'll make it right with Mark, even after I'm gone."

Her throat filled with emotion, but somehow she managed to choke out the words, "I'll try." She promised it because he seemed to need to hear it, even though the answer to that challenge might be outside of her control.

"Good," he said. "You're my mom, and I don't want you to be alone."

Blake's words continued to eat at Shannon, even after he went to bed and Mark returned home, stepping with her in a dance of awkwardness until she escaped to the safety of her car. How were they supposed to come back from their nasty argument when they couldn't even look each other in the eye?

She couldn't remember the drive from Mark's house to Hope Haven, and once she reached home, relieved Katie and locked up the house, she hurried upstairs to her room and closed herself inside. Her chest felt so tight that she couldn't draw a deep breath. She ached in a way that seemed to touch her spirit more than her body. She needed to be alone, the exact thing that her son feared for her future, but she needed time to think.

She slipped out of her clothes and into a pair of pink flannel pajamas. But even after she'd flipped off the bedside lamp and had snuggled under the covers, she couldn't shake the chill between her shoulder blades. She was surrounded by the girls she adored, by constant movement and chaos, but tonight it became clear to her just how alone she really was. She didn't want to be alone anymore. She wanted to be with Mark.

In her heart, Shannon knew that no matter how painful the things he'd said to her were, he was the only man who'd ever really known her. The only one who could make her happy. More than that, she realized now that so many of the things he'd said were true. Instead of taking responsibility for her mistakes, she'd blamed everyone else for them. How could her pregnancy have been her fault when it was Scott who'd taken advantage of her? Why should she have taken responsibility for her decisions when her parents had forced her to choose adoption?

Mark was right, too, that she expected him and Blake to forgive her, but she'd never forgiven her own parents or Blake's father for the ways they'd hurt her. She'd set out on a mission to earn Blake's forgiveness, when her

faith told her that forgiveness wasn't something someone earned or even deserved. It was a gift.

Suddenly, she remembered something else that Mark
had said. He'd reminded her of a scripture that talked
about forgiveness. As a new Christian, he hadn't committed a lot of verses to memory yet, but she was a
veteran of years of Sunday school and vacation Bible
school. She sat up in bed, turned on the lamp and
reached for her Bible. She had to flip through several
passages first, but finally she located Jesus' words in
Luke, chapter 6.

"'Do not judge, and you will not be judged,'" she
read at a whisper. "'Do not condemn, and you will not
be condemned. Forgive, and you will be forgiven.'"

It all sounded so easy, so straightforward, and yet
she'd failed in all of those areas. She'd judged, she'd
condemned and she'd held a grudge for fifteen years.

"Lord, I have failed You," she prayed aloud, her
words the only sounds besides the wind outside her
window. "And I've failed the others in my life. I haven't
forgiven them, and still I thought I deserved forgiveness. Please help me to forgive. And if Mark is the man
You have chosen for me, please show us the way to get
past the hurtful things we said. In Your name, amen."

Finally, she felt she could breathe again, her lungs
filling with oxygen as her heart expanded with hope.
Maybe there was a chance for her to restore her relationship with Mark after all. Tomorrow. She would go
to him and apologize again, and this time she would ask
for his forgiveness. She would offer him her forgiveness without expecting him to ask for it, and this time
she would really mean what she said. Then she would
tell him she wanted to be with him.

It might not be enough; she understood that. But then

she would have done everything she could. The rest was in God's hands, she thought, then smiled. It had been in His hands all along.

But before she could even think about a future with Mark, there was another relationship that she needed to address. One that had been wounded more than a decade before. One that appeared to have been healed on the outside but remained a badly patched-up break beneath the surface. She glanced at the clock. It was too late to call tonight. She frowned as she reached for the lamp switch, but she stopped her hand in midair.

Instead of turning off the light, she dropped her feet to the floor and reached for her cell phone after all. There was never a bad time to apologize. Never a wrong time to make things right. She made the call, waiting through several rings before someone finally answered. She took a deep breath and spoke.

"Hey, Dad, it's me."

Chapter Sixteen

"What are you doing up?" Mark asked from his spot in the dark when Blake descended the stairs. "You have school in the morning."

"It's Friday night, remember?"

"Oh. Right."

"And it's against the teenage code to go to bed on a Friday before eleven."

He blinked as Blake flipped on the side lamp, flooding the living room with light. He would have preferred to remain in the darkness with his thoughts, but he wasn't getting a vote. "I'll have to remember about the code."

He didn't mention that Blake had gone to bed early most nights since he'd been living there, particularly when he wanted to get away from the adults around him. Apparently he didn't need his space tonight.

"Do you want to join me?" Mark patted a place next to him on the sofa.

The boy stepped over to him, but he stopped in front of the couch and crossed his arms, staring down at Mark. It was clear that Blake had something to say, so instead of prodding, he settled back into the sofa cushions and waited. He didn't have to wait long.

"My mother's in love with you."

Mark blinked. He might have expected the boy to say a few things, but that wasn't one of them. "Blake, I'm sorry you've been put in an awkward position, but—"

"I just want to know one thing," Blake said to interrupt him.

He nodded. Maybe he didn't want to answer more questions about his almost relationship with Shannon, but Blake deserved that much. "What's that?"

"What are you going to do about it?"

"Look, you have to know that adult matters are complicated." He considered how awkward things had been between him and Shannon before she left tonight when, before, talking to her had been so easy. Too easy. Even after the apologies, all the wishes and prayers and even his plans to make a more permanent home for Blake, they just couldn't go back to the way things were before. He'd forgiven her, and she'd probably tried to forgive him, but would it ever be enough?

"It doesn't have to be complicated."

Mark shifted. He wanted to tell the boy that this was none of his concern, but Blake's mother *was* his business. "I don't know what you're trying to say."

Blake rolled his eyes in a way that he hadn't done for a few days at least and then flopped on the sofa but kept a buffer of space between them. "She loves you. You love her. So figure out a way to be with her."

Mark shook his head. "I don't know, buddy. As much as we might wish for it, some things can't be fixed."

"You're saying that to a guy who carried a letter with him for seven years and tracked down his birth mother at a home for teenage moms."

Mark chuckled, but the effort only made his chest ache. "I guess you're right."

"And I guess you must not want it—or her—that bad."

He squeezed his eyes shut at that, the ache spreading. "You'd be wrong about that," he said in low voice. "I love her, Blake."

"Then what are you going to do about it?" he said a second time.

What indeed? His heart told him one thing, while his head kept planting doubts. Did he have the courage to take the risk this time when he had nothing to lose and, possibly, so much to gain?

He didn't notice that Blake had stood again until he passed in front of him to the stairs and started climbing.

"Blake," he called. The boy turned to look over his shoulder. "Have you considered a career as a matchmaker?"

He shook his head. "Nah. I'm retiring now."

"And, Blake," he called after him again. "Thanks."

"No problem."

"Better get some sleep because I'll need you up bright and early."

Blake nodded, but he didn't ask any questions. Good thing because the plan was still forming in Mark's mind. Only one of them was going to get any sleep tonight. He had calls to make and schedules to coordinate, but more important than either of those things, he had to dig through the boxes in his basement. Somewhere down there, he had to locate a ring.

"Thank you so much for calling, Miss Lafferty. Yes, it's wonderful news."

Shannon managed to say goodbye and end the call

before she moaned out loud, but just barely. It was wonderful news, all right. It was the sweetest, most generous
gesture and an unfortunate offer, all rolled into one. She
set her cell phone on the desk and stared at it as if the
piece of electronic equipment were threatening to light
up again with another call. After receiving news that
changed everything *twice* this week in early-morning
phone calls, she planned to leave the thing turned off
tomorrow altogether.

Sure, Miss Lafferty was thrilled that Mark had volunteered to complete additional certification require-
ments to become Blake's long-term foster parent. And
Shannon really was grateful to him for ensuring that
Blake would continue to live nearby. But the situation
had become more complicated now that her plans for
obtaining custody were going against her.

Now if she told Mark that she wanted to build a life
with him, as she'd planned to do today, he would always
have to wonder if she'd just chosen him to be near her
son. How could she do that to the man she loved? Could
this be the answer she'd prayed for last night? But if
God didn't want them to be together, then why did the
thought of not being with him make her feel so empty?

Shannon was almost relieved when the doorbell rang,
even if it meant unannounced guests before breakfast on
a Saturday. It also offered an escape from emotions she
didn't want to feel, from thoughts she wasn't ready to
consider. She pushed up from her desk chair and started
out into the hall, where the girls, most still wearing pajamas, robes and slippers, scattered every which way.

"Are you going to answer it, Miss Shannon?" Kelly
asked.

"I guess so. None of you are dressed."

She, on the other hand, was already showered and

dressed, at least one benefit from a sleepless night. She supposed it didn't really matter whether the girls answered the door in their pajamas, as they were crowded behind her in the doorway anyway, unwilling to miss the morning's excitement.

Brushing her hand along her ponytail and straightening the hem of her long sweater, she finally opened the door. The crowd on her porch was so large that at first she couldn't make out any individuals from the group other than to note the sea of navy blue police uniforms. Her breath catching in her throat, she searched the many faces for answers.

What was going on? Had something happened to Blake? Or Mark? But the police didn't send a crowd to deliver bad news, did they? She scanned the drive where several patrol cars were parked. None of the red lights on top of the cars were lit, and none of the lights appeared to be spinning.

"What's going on, Miss Shannon?" one of the girls called from behind her.

"Why are all of the police here?"

"Are you in trouble?"

"No, I'm not in trouble," she said, responding to the one question for which she had an answer.

All of those bodies shifted to allow Mark and Blake, the only ones not in uniform, to move to the front of the crowd. It didn't make any sense. Both of them were smiling, too, which confused her even more. The idea struck her that maybe they were celebrating the news Miss Lafferty had just given her when Mark took a few steps closer.

"What's going on, Mark? What are you all doing here?"

He glanced over his shoulder at the men and women

behind him, his mouth lifting as he faced Shannon again.

"I told you some of my fellow troopers want to do some volunteer work at Hope Haven?"

She stared at him. None of this made sense. "You've come to do that now?"

He shook his head. "No. This is more of a social call."

Social call? They'd barely gotten beyond the awkwardness at just seeing each other the past few days, and he was making social calls?

"They're just along for the ride," Mark gestured widely to the wall of blue uniforms behind him. "It was Blake's idea."

"Oh, no." Blake shook his head. "Do you think I'd ever plan a party filled with badges? This was all him."

"Happy second Saturday of the Christmas shopping season," Trooper Davison called out, waving.

Mark rolled his eyes. "I wanted to make our visit a production this morning, and this was the best I could do on such short notice."

A production? She froze, waiting for him to explain. His words were still confusing, but a tiny part of her was tempted to hope. If he'd gone to so much trouble to make this a "production," then maybe one day in the far-off future, there might be a chance for them. Because she still stood in the open doorway, the freezing air pouring inside, one of the girls behind her approached with her coat, slipping it on her arms.

Shannon stepped closer to Mark and spoke in a low voice. "I wanted to thank you. Miss Lafferty told me what you did. It was so kind of you to offer to make a more permanent home for Blake, especially since... I can't."

"I did it for us," Mark whispered, only for her ears.

For us. Shannon blinked as the words reverberated in her head. There were still so many loose ends between them. So much to explain. Did this mean he'd really forgiven her? She was too afraid to tell herself that this could really be happening. Mark's gesture had already been the kindest thing anyone had ever done, and now it had become even more amazing. He'd done it for all of them.

Then in front of everyone, Mark lowered to one knee. Shannon stared at him, unable to move, unable to speak.

"Shannon, to say my whole life changed the day I met you and Blake would be an understatement. I've never felt more alive than I have since walking into your entertaining, messy world. Marry me, Shannon, and I'll work every day to make you as happy as you've made me."

But as he reached for her hand, she jerked both hands to her face instead. Her fingers were splayed over her eyes, her tears warm between them. Until Mark gently pulled her hands away from her eyes, she wasn't even aware that he'd stood again.

"Well, I was hoping for a happier response than that, especially with an audience, but—"

"I'm sorry, Mark. I'm sorry for so many things." She brushed quickly at her tears. "I don't know what to do."

"What to do?" He took her hands this time. "What do you mean? I don't want to push you, but I thought—"

Her words came out in a rush. "Of course I want to marry you. I love you. So much that sometimes I can't breathe. But how can I accept your proposal now that you'll be Blake's foster parent indefinitely? How can I make you always wonder if Blake was the only reason that I would want to be with you?"

Out of air now, she gulped in a hitched breath. Would he change his mind? She closed her eyes, knowing whatever he would say now would alter both of their lives forever.

At the sound of Mark's chuckle, she opened her eyes. He squeezed her hands.

"Well, *is* he the only reason?"

"No." She shook her head for emphasis. "I love you. I want to be with you."

He smiled. "Then that's good enough for me."

Again Mark kneeled in front of her, and this time he pulled a ring from his pocket. A round diamond with smaller stones on each side.

"It's my mother's ring," he said as she looked down at it. "I've never given it to anyone else. It was all I could come up with on short notice, but if you'd prefer something else…"

She stared into his eyes. "It's perfect."

Mark cleared his throat. "I'm going to try this again. Shannon, will you be my wife and help me build a family for Blake?"

This time she grinned, her tears forgotten. "I'd like to see you try to stop me."

"I should have gone with the ring the first time," Mark remarked as he came to his feet.

He earned a laugh, but he wasn't paying attention to their audience. His gaze was on Shannon alone. He reached for her, pulling her slowly toward him. She smiled and went willingly into his arms. His kiss felt like a promise made and kept, a dream offered and accepted. Applause broke out all around them, but he kept on kissing her. She was dazed when he finally moved away, but Mark only reached for Blake, pulling him into a family hug. Blake pretended to hate all of that gushy emotion, but none of them bought it.

"Miss Shannon's getting married," one of the girls called out from behind Shannon in a singsong voice.

Trooper Davison stepped closer to them and shivered. "Are you guys done now? Can we go inside? It's freezing out here."

"Oh. Right." Shannon turned back to the crowd. "Everybody come inside. Breakfast for everyone."

More laughter followed, but when Shannon pulled the door wide, more than a dozen ruddy-faced adults squeezed inside the entry. Her parents were the last two to pass through the door.

Shannon's mouth went slack when she saw them. "Mom and Dad, I didn't even know you were here."

Marilyn grinned as she lowered her hood. "We stayed to the back."

"It's cold, all right," Roger said, pulling a stocking cap off his head.

As the girls and Blake led the rest of the guests into the cafeteria area, Mark and Shannon hung back with her parents.

"How did this happen?" Shannon gestured widely to Mark and her parents.

Mark grinned. "I called them early this morning and invited them. I was hoping it would give you the chance to apologize to them, but, according to them, you'd already taken care of that."

She reached for Mark's hand and squeezed it. The man who'd already done so much for her had reached out to her parents, as well.

Shannon hugged her mother first and then her father. "You have to be tired after being up so late last night talking to me. I'm really glad you're here."

Marilyn hugged her daughter again. "We've missed too much already. Of our daughter's life. Of our grandson's life." She paused to wipe away tears from the corners of her eyes. "We wouldn't have missed this for the world."

Shannon reached a thumb to wipe away a tear her mother had missed. "I wouldn't miss it, either."

Epilogue

Shannon smoothed the skirt of her ivory silk sheath wedding gown and stared at herself in her bureau mirror. It had to have been the fastest three-week engagement known to man, but to her it felt too long, anyway. Although she didn't want to wait any longer than necessary to be Mark's wife, they'd had to schedule the wedding as far away from any of the girls' due dates as possible, and the Saturday after Christmas had worked out perfectly. They even had the chance to use the great Christmas decorations in the parlor at Hope Haven, from the huge Douglas fir tree to the lovely crèche.

She was just adjusting the comb of her fingertip veil into her updo when she heard a knock at the door.

"Come in."

Kelly pushed the door open and stepped inside, with Chelsea and Holly trailing behind her.

"Oh, look at you, Miss Shannon." Kelly brushed her fingers lovingly over the lace of the veil. "You make such a pretty bride."

"Beautiful," Chelsea said.

"Gorgeous," Holly agreed.

"You ladies look wonderful, too."

And they did. Holly wore red taffeta, Chelsea looked sweet in violet sateen and Kelly couldn't stop spinning in the pink lace. Finding a wedding gown on short notice had been simple compared to the challenge of locating eleven pretty maternity dresses from resale shops all over Oakland and Livingston counties. Shannon couldn't get over that her parents had offered to pay for the whole wedding, including the eleven bridesmaids' dresses. They'd wanted to do it for their only daughter and only grandson.

"You'll all make pretty brides someday, too," Shannon assured them. "And I had better receive an invitation to each of your weddings."

With their assurances and a few tears, they all crowded around the mirror to fix their makeup.

"Well, Trooper Shoffner said it's time for all of us to come down," Chelsea told her.

"You know, you can call him Mark when he's not at work," Shannon told them.

"How about Mr. Mark?" Kelly asked.

"I'm sure he would like that."

The girls led the way down the stairs, where they joined the other bridesmaids, all looking lovely and grown-up in their gowns. Beyond them, her father stood with Blake, both appearing equally uncomfortable in their simple black suits. As Shannon slipped in next to them, Blake drew her aside.

"You make an amazing bride, Miss Shannon. I'm happy for you. For us." He leaned in and dropped a kiss on her cheek. "I love you, Mom."

Her eyes immediately flooded. "I love you, too."

Her father came to the rescue with a handkerchief, which Shannon used to dab her eyes. Blake tried to be discreet, brushing at the corners of his eyes.

A recording of a wedding processional started to play, so they all took their places. It only seemed right that both Blake and her father would escort her down the aisle—two of the three guys she loved the most, leading her to the third. The girls made their way up the makeshift aisle first. By the time Shannon, her father and Blake reached the entry, the area near the lectern was so full that the line of girls curled along the opposite wall.

Besides those colorful dresses and the red bows, garland and the twinkling lights of the Christmas decorations, the color that dominated the room was state police navy blue.

Shannon took note of the other guests, her mother in a light gray suit and Brooke, who attended with her mother and father. Her baby would be released from the hospital in the next few days.

Finally, she caught sight of Mark on the right side of the lectern, looking so handsome and strong in his dress uniform. His two brothers stood behind him in their dark suits, supporting him just like she'd assured him they would.

Her gaze connected with Mark's, and it felt as if there was no one else in the room but them. Before she'd met him she'd thought she knew what love was, but it had only been a pale imitation to this emotion that joined their hearts and would soon join the two of them for life. She didn't even realize that her father and Blake had started walking, leading her forward, until she drew near Mark and her father placed her hand in his.

Reverend Hicks stepped to the lectern and opened his Bible. "Friends, we are gathered here in the sight of God and these witnesses to unite Mark and Shannon in holy matrimony…."

She tried, really tried, to listen to the rest of the words he said, but only fragments—"God instituted marriage," "faith, hope and love,"—filtered through her thoughts. All she could see was the man standing before her, offering her his heart and his life.

"Now, Shannon, repeat after me. 'I, Shannon, take you, Mark, to be my lawfully wedded husband,'" the minister said.

She repeated the words, feeling confident and strong, and then listened in awe as Mark repeated his vows. Soon Mark was slipping that gold band on her finger, and she was doing the same for him.

"And now I pronounce you husband and wife," Reverend Hicks said. "You may kiss the bride."

"I would be happy to," Mark announced as he leaned forward and brushed his lips over hers.

As soon as he pulled back, Mark glanced to the line of folding chairs. "Yo, Blake, get over here."

The boy rolled his eyes, but he stepped over to join them. Together the three of them, holding hands, led the guests from the parlor into the cafeteria for the reception. Shannon leaned over and pressed a kiss to Blake's cheek and then turned her head the other way, sharing a kiss with the most amazing man she'd ever known. Her husband.

What had begun as an alliance for the sake of one troubled boy had become so much more. Only in accepting the roles they'd played in their own pain had she and Mark finally found the healing they'd craved. They still had a long road ahead of them as the courts determined Blake's permanent custody, but Shannon had no fear of the journey ahead. Her new life had come in the form of two surprise visitors on her doorstep. Now that life would be the most wonderful gift she'd never known she wanted: the three of them…together.

* * * * *

Dear Reader,

Forgiveness tends to be a recurring theme in my books. Of course, forgiveness is central to the Christian life as well, for without it we would have no hope. But I believe I regularly force my characters to take on this tough subject for another reason. Because I'm so bad at it in my own life. When someone hurts one of my girls, my talons come out, and I can hold a grudge with the best of them. Anyone who dares to injure one of them doesn't deserve forgiveness anyway, right?

But that's the whole point with God's forgiveness. Neither earned nor deserved, it is a gift. Challenging or not, He expects us to forgive each other, too. "And be kind one to another, tenderhearted, forgiving each other, just as God in Christ has forgiven you." Ephesians 4:32.

It is always a treat to hear from readers, so I encourage you to contact me through email at danacorbit@earthlink.net, snail mail at P.O. Box 5, Novi, MI 48376, find me on Facebook or follow me on Twitter @DanaCorbit1.

Dana Corbit

Questions for Discussion

1. From whom did Shannon say her parents wanted to keep her pregnancy a secret? Why do we often fear judgment from the very people we should trust most to support us?

2. What did Blake offer as proof that Shannon was his mother?

3. What was the one event in Mark's youth over which he believed his parents always judged him? How do the mistakes of our youth affect the adults we become?

4. What did most of the teens at Hope Haven have in common besides their pregnancies?

5. Shannon had always planned to find Blake when he turned eighteen. Should birth parents reach out to the children they placed for adoption?

6. Why was Mark so desperate to build a decorated career with the Michigan State Police?

7. Why did Brooke attempt to hide the symptoms that sent her to the hospital on Thanksgiving Day?

8. What issue did Shannon recognize in Blake that made it more difficult for him to be placed in a foster home?

9. What did Mark and Shannon share in common that stood as a stumbling block for them to build a future together?

10. After Shannon spent much of the story trying to earn Blake's forgiveness, what did she realize about God's forgiveness?

11. Who was the only person who refused to forgive Mark for the mistakes of his past?

12. How did Shannon betray both the man she loved and her own son in her attempt to punish her parents for pressuring her into choosing adoption?

COMING NEXT MONTH FROM
Love Inspired®

Available April 15, 2014

HER UNLIKELY COWBOY
Cowboys of Sunrise Ranch
by Debra Clopton
Widow Suzie Kent needs help dealing with her troubled teenage son. Can tough sheriff Tucker McDermott prove he's the perfect man for the job?

JEDIDIAH'S BRIDE
Lancaster County Weddings
by Rebecca Kertz
When Jedidiah Lapp saves her brothers' lives, Sarah Mast quickly falls for the kind, strong hero. But when he must return to his own community, will they ever meet again?

NORTH COUNTRY MOM
Northern Lights
by Lois Richer
Alicia Featherstone never thought she'd have a family of her own. But she can see a future with former detective Jack Campbell and his adorable daughter...if she can make peace with her past.

LOVING THE LAWMAN
Kirkwood Lake
by Ruth Logan Herne
She vowed she'd never fall for another lawman, but when widow Gianna Costanza meets handsome deputy sheriff Seth Campbell, he could be the man she breaks her promise for.

THE FIREMAN FINDS A WIFE
Cedar Springs
by Felicia Mason
Summer Spencer knows it's risky to fall for a man with a dangerous job. But how can she resist falling for charming firefighter Cameron Jackson when he's melting her heart?

FOREVER HER HERO
by Belle Calhoune
Coast Guard hero Sawyer Trask has loved his childhood friend Ava for as long as he can remember. Will their second chance at love be destroyed by a painful secret?

_____

LICNM0414

REQUEST YOUR FREE BOOKS!

2 FREE INSPIRATIONAL NOVELS

PLUS 2 FREE MYSTERY GIFTS

Love Inspired

LI13R

SPECIAL EXCERPT FROM

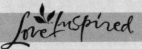

Widowed mom Suzie Kent is desperate to help her troubled son. Is her only hope the man she blames for her husband's death?

Read on for a preview of
HER UNLIKELY COWBOY by Debra Clopton,
Book #3 in the SUNRISE RANCH series.

"Suzie Kent. It's good to see you." Tucker McDermott's eyes crinkled around the edges, but concern stamped his expression, as if he knew the dismay shooting through her.

Her breath had flown from her lungs and she had no words as she looked into the face of the man she held responsible for her husband's death.

The man she was also counting on to help her save her son.

The man she wasn't prepared to see, though she'd just driven three hours with a moving van and plans to live on Sunrise Ranch, the ranch his family owned and operated.

Her world tilted as she realized whose clean, tangy aftershave was teasing her senses and whose unbelievably intense gaze had her insides suddenly rioting. His hair was jet-black and his skin deeply tanned, making his deep blue eyes startling in their intensity.

"Tucker," she managed, hoping her voice didn't wobble.

Moving to Dew Drop, Texas, to Tucker's family's Sunrise Ranch, asking for his help, had taken everything she had left emotionally—and that hadn't been much, since her husband had given his life in the line of duty for fellow marine Tucker two years earlier.

Tucker grimaced, trying to keep most of his weight off Suzie and Abe, but his hip clearly hurt.

"Thank y'all for helping me," he said, his gaze snagging on hers again and holding. "I've got it from here, though." He pulled one arm from around her and the other from around her son, Abe.

"Are you sure?" she asked, even though she wanted to step away from him in the worst way. "Do we need to get you to your vehicle?

Tucker limped a few painful steps away from them. "I'm okay," he said gruffly. "It'll just take a few minutes for the throbbing to go away." He glanced ruefully at the donkeys on the road. "What a mess. They act like they own the road."

Abe chuckled. "They sure took you out."

"By the way, I'm Tucker McDermott. I was a friend of your dad's and I owe him my life. He was an amazing man." Tucker cleared his throat. "I'm glad you've come to Dew Drop. And the boys of Sunrise Ranch are looking forward to meeting you."

Will this cowboy heal her family—and her heart?

Pick up HER UNLIKELY COWBOY to find out.
Available May 2014
wherever Love Inspired® Books are sold.